The Sin Eater's Prince

By

Keta Diablo

About The Sin Eater's Prince

A Gay Romance Vampire Novel

Physician Andras Maddock has never shunned Owen, the Sin Eater of the village. How can he ignore the man he loves? Owen is stunned when Andras saves him from a gruesome death at the hands of vampire. How did a simple man acquire supernatural strength?

Dagan, Dark Lord of the Underworld, vows to take the mystic sword from Andras, a weapon that allows his vampires to tolerate sunlight. Dagan will do anything to avenge his father's death and make the Sin Eater his slave.

"In the midst of life we are in death."

Ynghanol ein bywyd, yr ydym yn angau

Welsh Words and Their Meaning

Abergwaun: A town in Wales
Annwn: Heaven, the other world of youthful delights
Coblynau: Troll-like beings, miners
Cŵn Annwn: The black hounds of Hell
Cwth: A fiddle
Diawl:The devil
Draig: Dragon
Dyn Hysbys: A wizard
Glyndŵr: Welsh rebel
Gwyllion: Female faires with frightful characteristics
Gwrach y Rhibyn: The Hag of the Mist
Iolo Gocha: Court poet
Lladd amser: Killing Time
Nos Galan Gaeaf: The night the spirits walk the land
Owain ap Gruffydd Fychan: Prince of Wales full name
(warlord
Sin Eater: A sin-eater is a person who consumes a ritual
meal in order to spiritually take on the sins of a
deceased person. Sin-eaters, as a consequence, carried
the sins of all people whose sins they had eaten.
Cultural anthropologists and folklorists classify sin-
eating as a form of ritual.
Tad: Father
Tatws-a-llaeth: Potatoes and buttermilk
Tylwyth Teg: The Fae or fairy people
Tywysog Cymru: Prince of Wales, 1400
Uffern: Hell
Wdig: A town in Wales

Table of Contents

Chapter One

Pembrokeshire, Southwest Wales
1842

Someone would die today.
The inexplicable forewarning pulsed through Owen's veins. His tad had the same gift, or was it a curse bequeathed to all sin eaters? He didn't want to dwell on his sire's passing four years ago, or think about the oppressive mantle he'd inherited when the man the town folk called Halwn drew his last breath.

He'd rather stand on his summit and devour the magnificent view, watch the ocean crash into shore. Nestled between the brow of the peak and the town of Wdig, his father's land belonged to him now. If one could say land belonged to man. Like many mornings, he studied the bustle of activity from the town below. He knew most of the villagers by sight. The dour-faced Widow McKee, broom in hand, shooed sand from her stoop, the lass known as Bridget toted pails of fresh milk to her cottage and neighbors Alden Alistair lent an ear to Duncan Moore over the picket fence between their properties. He'd never lived in the village, wouldn't be welcomed in Wdig or the neighboring village of Abergwaun. Deemed unholy, sin eaters had been shunned by town folk for centuries.

Over his shoulder, the goats whined a chorus of bleats, competing with the throaty calls of the wood warblers. With a sigh, he turned from the panoramic view. He'd return in a few hours, watch the sea gulls soar along the long stretch of coastal marsh, or look west to the moors, a treeless stretch of land blanketed in dense bracken and wild heather. He loved his meager parcel of Duw's earth. Other than his goats and fiddle, the land was all he had.

Childbed fever took his mother at his birth, which meant he'd never felt a woman's gentle touch or had the pleasure of a sibling's companionship. His life had been filled with nevers. And solitude.

An outcrop of yews along the steep path to his abode rustled. Since he'd awakened with a premonition of someone's death, he expected a visitor soon.

A mass of copper tresses glistened when Carys appeared on the crest. "Good morn, Owen."

"Ye' are about early, lass."

Huffing after the steep climb, the young woman drew several deep breaths. "Doctor Maddock sent me for a pint of goat milk. Mrs. Bellamy's babe has the appetite of an ogre."

"A shame the woman died giving birth."

"I christened him Ifan. Does the name agree with ye?"

He shrugged. "I didn't get a good look at the boy, but 'tis a suitable name."

"I thought ye might know what it means."

Owen walked to the pen, released the latch, and stepped inside. The goats meandered toward his familiar stool and the shiny, silver pail. "Mayhap he should have been named after his sire."

Carys wrinkled her small nose. "The man cares nothing for the child. 'Tis doubtful his sire has seen anything but the bottom of a tankard since his beloved Fanny died."

"What if one day he claims the lad?" Finished milking the first goat, Owen patted his rump and went to work on the second. "What will your heart say to that?"

A frown bowed her pretty mouth. "'Twould be too broken to speak."

"Ye should not attach yourself to the lad, Carys."

She nodded, but he knew his admonition had fallen on deaf ears. The lass was kind-hearted, too kind-hearted at times. Owen milked the spotted goat with the ragged ears and came to his feet. "Wait here. I'll fill a pint and ye can be on your way."

"Andras says ye are to bring the milk, return with me."

"Oh, he does, does he? How many years have ye been doing his bidding now?"

"Ye know full well I don't do his bidding, Owen. I have helped him minister to the sick and dying for... well, for as long as I can remember."

"I awoke knowing it."

"Knowing what?"

"That someone would die soon."

"Are ye familiar with the cobbler from Abergwaun, Clough the elder?"

Owen nodded.

"'Tis rumored he'll not last through sunset." She paused. "His wife has called for the sin eater. Andras says ye should bring the milk and tickle two feet with one feather."

A smile tugged his lips. Carys' peculiar speech and strange superstitions amused him. Other than Andras Maddock, the lass had been the only human to show him kindness.

"Very well. I still must fill the pint before we journey down."

Her lovely face took on a contemplative expression.

"What is it, lass?"

"Do ye think Mistress Bellamy walked over a grave while carrying Ifan?"

"I don't abide by superstitious nonsense and ye would be wise not to."

"During the babe's christening, his head fell back

into the arms holding him."

"What is the meaning of such an event?"

Green eyes narrowed. "He might live to a ripe old age had he kept his head up."

Owen shook his head and held back a laugh. "Tis time ye stop believing in foolish tales, Carys. After the babe's harrowing birth, he lacked the strength to keep his head up."

Owen followed her eyes while she inspected his humble surroundings—the dilapidated wooden abode, a bowed-roof lean-to and decrepit goat pen. Bringing her scrutiny to an end, she caught his eyes again. "Do ye ever hear the faeries sing?" Without waiting for an answer, she continued. "Or monsters, giants, magicians, other creatures of the enchantment?"

"Ye think the Land of Faeries my neighbors, the home of the Tylwyth Teg?"

She nodded. "What say ye about the Coblynau who are said to haunt the mines and quarries? Is it true they stand one foot tall, are hideous and unsightly?"

He gave a dramatic shudder. "Revolting enough to scare the mustache off a hare."

"Don't tease me. I know hares don't have mustaches." A pensive look wrinkled her brow. "The elders claim ye live amid the green meadows of enchantment."

"Do they now?"

"Aye. Do ye?"

"I've seen the Gwyllion on occasion, female fairies of frightful characteristics. 'Tis said they haunt the lonely roads of the mountains to lead night-wanderers astray."

Her eyes grew wide for a moment and then narrowed again when he winked. "Oh, ye are spiteful, Owen Rhys. My time is squandered talking to ye about the fae and enchantment." An exasperated sigh left her lips. "I'll not walk with ye down the hill. Deliver the pint before midday, and mayhap ye should prepare to spend the night. Sire Clough has one foot in this world, one in the afterlife."

"Tell Doctor Maddock I'll bring the milk and remain until Clough passes."

She turned and called out over her shoulder. "If the Gwyllion take me, will be on your head."

"Carys, wait!"

With questioning eyes, she faced him. "Aye?"

"Most avoid me as they would a leper. Do ye not fear me?"

Her smile dazzled him. "I don't abide by such superstitions and ye'd be wise not to, Owen Rhys."

She bounded off, a lively tune on her lips and her long, russet hair swaying against her slender back. Carys' life mirrored his somewhat. Andras Maddock took her in after her parents were murdered. Villagers found their remains in the woods, their throats ripped out, and their limbs severed from their bodies.

Werewolves with eyes of fire, the elders claimed. 'The lycanthrope journey from Pembroke Castle on occasion and haunt the shadowy domains of the forest.' Owen didn't know if the tales held merit or were the superstitious babblings of men after consuming large tankards of ale. He didn't care to find out.

Carys was ten years of age when her parents passed. She considered Andras her only kin now. Owen envied the girl's good fortune in that regard. What he wouldn't give to gaze upon the physician every hour of every day.

A visit to the man's elegant dwelling served as a dismal reminder of his own beggarly life. He didn't have a prayer of elevating his station. Once his sire passed, he had two choices before him, follow in his tad's footsteps or starve.

He no longer cared what the town folk thought of his miserable existence. He'd grown accustomed to their brash stares and ill-mannered remarks. Andras Maddock was another matter. The physician had never looked at him in an uncivil manner. On the contrary, the man's dove-gray eyes held kindness and an unnamed emotion Owen couldn't decipher. Andras didn't have the slightest inkling his nearness threatened to destroy the restraint Owen held in control. How could the man know he ignited a fire in his blood that could never be fanned to life? The physician dazzled him. He could think of no other word for what he felt toward the man.

None of the lasses from the village had ever granted him as much as a g'day, but at twenty-five years of age, shouldn't he be wishing they would? Therein lay the problem. Not one fair-headed, long-limbed girl sent his pulse racing or caused his heart to thunder against his ribs. That euphoria was reserved for Andras.

"Nine shames on ye, Owen! Ye are nobody, destined to a life of carnal wonderings, longing for the caress of Andras's hands." After his outburst, the doe looked his way with soulful eyes. He patted her flank and continued his tirade. "Ye lust after a man who doesn't know ye exist. If he did, he'd run fast and far to find out ye craved his look, his touch." He rose from the stool and plucked the full pail of milk from the ground. "Duw, help me. Is it not enough I must wear the heavy mantle of a sin eater, but must I covet what I can never have?"

After changing into clean corduroy trousers—the one pair he owned—a fresh linen shirt and a leather jerkin, Owen set off for Abergwaun with a pint of milk tucked under his arm.

He'd avoid the main thoroughfare of his village, head east along the coast until he arrived at the back side of the brickworks in lower town Abergwaun. Once he climbed the steep cliff to upper town, he'd have to pass through the marketplace and village shops to reach Maddock Manor.

He wouldn't be assaulted, merely ignored. A beating would be preferable to abhorrence in his opinion, but the inhabitants would rather sell their souls than acknowledge, much less touch, a sin eater.

Following the sun's brilliant rays, Owen stopped at the top of Maddock's summit and took in the breathtaking view of the sea. The man shared the scene with a church and all shape and manner of houses near the common center. He drew a deep breath, turned, and walked through the crowded market with his head down, not bothering to glance at the residents bustling in and out of the quaint shops.

The stately manor loomed before him, its pristine white shutters and matching pillars glistening under golden streaks of light. Reaching for the brass knocker, he lifted it and rapped three times.

The tread of light footsteps reached him from the other side and then the door opened. Carys greeted him with a smile and a flourish of her arm toward the foyer. "Come, Andras awaits ye in his study."

A shiver of anticipation sent goose bumps rippling along his skin and he hadn't even laid eyes on the man yet. If only he could leave his wanton desire at the door stoop. He followed Carys into the study where Andras sat behind a large mahogany desk.

Rising from the chair, Andras skirted the desk and extended his hand toward the pint of milk. "Thank ye for coming, Owen."

He nodded and met his eyes, captivated by the power of his stare. Why did they always seem to shimmer in incandescent hues of scarlet? The room loomed dark, like the entire house. He'd never been inside Maddock Manor when it hadn't been cast in muted shades of gray. The heavy brocade draperies met in the middle, blocking out the sun, and the lanterns had been turned down. Behind him, the door eased shut and Carys' footsteps echoed down the hallway.

The air between him and Andras hummed with the usual undercurrents, but Owen never knew whether the awkwardness stemmed from his social ineptness or from another unknown source.

Across the room, Andras's eyes narrowed. "Carys told ye about Bevan Clough?"

"She did," he managed to eke out.

"I expect the man will leave us this night." The deep timbre of Andras's voice whispered over him, eliciting images that refused to leave his head.

"May Duw welcome him," he said willing the erotic visions to leave. "I'm prepared to stay in the stables until morn."

The gray eyes softened. "Ye will stay in the manor, in a room I've prepared for—"

"No, 'twould be unseemly."

A dark brow rose. "In what regard?"

"The presence of a sin eater in the manor would cast aspersions—"

"I'm lord of my manor." His mesmerizing voice filled the warm space between their bodies. "No man tells me who I might host under my own roof."

Owen breathed out a sigh. "I can't stay in the manor. 'Tis for one night, and I'm accustomed to lesser quarters."

"More than one night, I fear. Mistress Davies also courts death, although I expect her to linger a day or two." He took the pint of milk to his desk, attempted to remove the stopper and met resistance. "It makes little sense for ye to return to Wdig on the morrow only to make the journey again the following day."

The woman would die within the day, two at best. He'd felt the cold winds of death nudge his soul on two occasions of late. He didn't know who'd die but sensed the dark foreboding, as his father and grandfather had. Intent on assisting him with the stopper, Owen walked toward him. "Let me help ye with...."

To his surprise, the stopper separated from the bottle, carrying with it an inch or two of glass. Andras's hand crashed into the jagged top of the pint and he grimaced. "Argh! Now I shall have to strain the milk through a cloth to be certain the babe doesn't ingest bits of glass."

Owen looked about the room for a cloth to stop the blood flow, shocked to discover not a drop oozed from the wound. He stood close enough to see the cut—the deep separation of skin—but not a dribble of blood appeared along the ragged tear.

When their eyes met, Andras reached into the pocket of his vest, pulled out a linen handkerchief, and clamped it over the wound. "'Tis not but a scratch, nothing to fret over."

His father's last words echoed in his mind. "Beware of the long tooth, son."

The faint red glow in Andras's eyes, the gloomy manor, and now the lack of blood set off warning bells in his head. Dazed by the likelihood, Owen took a step back with the word *vampire* roaring through his head.

"If ye insist on retiring with the beasts, see my man Bellamy, and he'll supply ye with a blanket."

"Very well, Doctor Maddock. I'll be on my way then. If ye need me for anything, ye will find me in the stables."

He stared at the handkerchief covering the wound, his brow creased.

"Aye, if I hear anything from the Cloughs, I'll summon ye."

Owen turned, headed for the door and repressed a shiver. On the way to the stables, he wondered if the shiver was a result of being in the exquisite man's presence or because he'd just held a conversation with a long tooth?

Chapter Two

A lantern near the door provided the meager light in Andras's stables. From his pile of hay in an empty stall, Owen clutched the woolen blanket and rolled to his side. He'd dissected the events in Andras's study a hundred times and stood no closer now to solving the mystery than he had hours ago.

He thought about his father's last days on earth. On his deathbed, the man had rambled about Welsh legend and lore, but Owen expected nothing less from the dyed-in-the-wool Welshman. Diphtheria had ravaged his body, the resultant fever addling his sharp brain. He blathered about *Nos Galan Gaeaf*, the night the spirits walk the land and the night the tail-less black sow comes to steal the living.

Andras had arrived at their dwelling in a vain attempt to save him, but departed at sunrise with a somber face and a shake of his long black hair. Afterward, his father had spewed endlessly about vampires, werewolves and other beastly creatures roaming the desolate lakes and mountain heights of Pembrokeshire.

"Beware of the long tooth, son," he'd said, his pale blue eyes fixed on the door. He'd spoken other words, freezing the blood in Owen's veins. "Lladd amser." Owen had seldom heard the words for *Killing Time*, but there could be no mistake in their meaning or the dire warning from his father's trembling lips.

Unable to sleep now, Owen rose from his bed of straw, believing a brisk walk around the massive interior might bring him respite. After tossing a woolen blanket his way, Bellamy, Andras's blade smith, had long ago retired to his modest cottage on the property.

Drawn to Bellamy's forge and an array of the

smithy's tools—tongs, hammer and anvil—Owen's gaze drifted to a large chest sitting katy-corner to the man's slack tub. An ornate, oak trunk beckoned him. Well-crafted, it seemed out of place in such a rough-hewn setting. He dropped to his knees and stared at the wrought-iron clasp for several long moments before attempting to lift the lid. To his surprise, it wasn't locked.

A length of luxurious black silk hid the contents from view, heightening his curiosity. Pulling back a corner of the fabric, a short gasp of awe found him. There lay a sword. Not just any sword, but a weapon that would be the envy of every soldier and warlord in Wales. Owen looked over his shoulder to ensure no one had entered the stables, and then plucked the rapier from its secret grave. Laying it flat in his hands, he estimated the length to be over forty inches, the weight close to ten pounds.

On one side of the guard were the words *Tywysog Cymru*, Prince of Wales, 1400-16, and around the pommel was the full name of the warlord, *Owain ap Gruffydd Fychan*.

Owen's heart slowed to a heavy thud. Why would Andras be in possession of Glyndŵr's renowned sword? Latent memories of schooling from his father surfaced. Seated at the trestle table, and reading by lamplight, the elderly sin eater had read to him every night, his tedious lessons on Welsh history placing him into a snore at times.

"Our beloved Prince instigated the revolt against Henry IV of England over four hundred years ago," he'd said, pointing to a colorful depiction in a book. "'Tis true his army was put down, but not without triumph." Owen had asked at the time if the Prince of Wales died during the uprising. "Nay, but Glyndŵr disappeared, was never captured or betrayed. Some say he's buried on the land once owned by his children, but 'tis a secret. "The precious gems on the hilt winked at Owen, returning him to the present. He came to his feet, hefted the sword over his head and sliced through the stagnant air of the barn. A chuckle followed on the heels of his inept thrust. The sword was more than half his height in length, and him inexperienced, a casual observer would deem him a clumsy oaf for brandishing the weapon in such a manner.

He stooped and returned the rapier to the chest, the niggling questions about Andras more befuddling than before. The man emanated danger, lethal danger. It frightened and thrilled him.

Andras's voice echoed in the spacious chamber. "Owen? Why are ye not asleep?"

Turning to face him with his heart beating like a captured wren and a stutter falling from his lips, he met Andras's piercing gaze. "I-I thought I heard a noise coming from the forge."

Andras studied him for a long moment before speaking. "Mistress Clough calls for the sin eater."

He brushed the remnants of straw from his clothing and ran a hand through his tousled hair. "The elder has passed?"

"If not, he'll depart soon."

Under a star-fading sky, Owen kept pace with Andras's long strides as they descended the steep hill and made their way to the Clough's residence in lower town. Outside their abode, a handful of watchers stood ready--men who'd do their best in the next two days to raise Clough from the dead and in the process affirm the man had passed on to the afterlife.

Owen followed Andras through the door and into the kitchen where the elderly man's corpse was laid out on the table. The new widow, sons, daughters and grandchildren surrounded his body, their mournful cries and prayers drifting toward the rafters of the meek dwelling.

The rotund, gray-haired wife looked up upon their entrance, walked to the cupboard and returned with a mazar bowl of ale and a loaf of bread. She placed the loaf on her husband's abdomen and reached across the corpse, handing Owen the bowl of ale with one hand, dropping a six-pence into his palm with the other.

She dabbed her red-rimmed eyes with the corner of her white apron and looked to Andras. "Will ye not pronounce him dead, sir?"

Andras placed two fingers against his neck, leaned over his body and closed his eyes. Moments later, he lifted his head and nodded. "He's gone."

A strangled sob left the woman's throat. "According to my husband's last wishes, instruct the sin eater to assume his transgressions."

When Andras turned to him with a nod, Owen stepped up to the table with the ale in his hand. He put the bowl to his lips and emptied it. Next, he picked up the bread from the man's torso, broke off several pieces from the crusty loaf and chewed. The room fell silent.

"I give easement and rest now to thee, Bevan Clough," he whispered. "Come not down the lanes or in our meadows. And for thy peace, I pawn my own soul. Amen."

His head bowed with his eyes cast upon the dead man, Owen stuffed the last of the bread into his mouth and chewed. A chorus of wails erupted in the room and the widow fell upon her husband's chest. Owen took a step back, his eyes drawn to the limpid, gray mist escaping the man's mouth.

He recalled the first time he saw a soul leave the body. At the young age of eleven, he'd accompanied his father to the parish house where the parson was abed, the death rattle wheezing from his chest. After the man breathed his last, and while his father stood over him partaking of the dead cakes, the man's soul slipped from his open mouth and disappeared skyward, like smoke up a chimney.

"We know not who is there to meet his soul," his father had said that evening. "'Tis for Duw and Diawl to fight over."

"Do the others not see his soul leave?" he'd asked.

"Nay, they do not wish to see."

Andras nudged his arm, breaching his memories. "Our duties are done; let us be on our way."

Dragging his feet through town, Owen had difficulty keeping up with Andras's brisk pace. The man had speed; he'd allow him that. By the time they reached the bottom of the steep knoll, Owen drew a deep breath and gathered his strength. A lack of sleep and the unsettling aspects of his duties contributed to his weariness.

Andras led the way up the rugged crag, looking over his shoulder now and then to see if he followed. Owen lumbered up the hill—he could only think of it as lumbering compared to Andras's graceful strides—and focused on the moonlit path, matching Andras's every footprint with one of his own. He had an uncanny feeling the nimble doctor would have reached the summit by now left to his own devices.

An owl screamed overhead, shattering Owen's concentration. He lost his footing, clutched a nearby branch and groaned when it slipped from his grasp. Tumbling backwards, his knees rolled over his shoulders in rapid succession and swallowed up the ground he'd just ascended. A dull thud reached his ears and a white-hot pain shot through him when his head made contact with the rock he'd used as a stepping stone minutes ago.

Coming to an abrupt halt, he lifted his battered

body into a sitting position with a moan that seemed to come from outside his body. He looked up and imagined a cloaked hunter riding through the night sky. Wavering between lucidity and the dream world, Andras's dark visage floated before him, powerful and sure. His dazed brain registered the improbability—how had the man appeared so suddenly?

The stars shifted and then a black veil enveloped him.

* * *

Owen awoke to strange surroundings. A heather-scented pillow comforted his throbbing head and fine linen bed sheets rustled beneath him. *I've died and entered heaven.*

"No, ye haven't left the earth, Owen. I brought ye into the manor after the fall knocked ye senseless."

His pulse beat a painful rhythm near his temples when he snapped his head toward the voice. He hadn't said the words aloud, he was certain of it, and yet Andras knew what he'd been thinking. He rolled his legs toward the edge of the bed and attempted to rise.

"Do not leave that bed, Owen! Ye took a hard blow and I've stitched the torn flesh at the back of your head. Ye must remain abed for the day."

He didn't want to stay in Andras's house. It reminded him of everything he lacked in life...and everything he desired, notwithstanding the mere presence of the man left him weak-kneed and tongue-tied.

"I can't stay; I must return...." The room spun and he felt his eyes roll back in his head. Andras bolted from his chair beside the bed and eased him back onto the pillow.

"Ye are safe here, Owen. No harm will come to ye."

A shiver coursed through him.

"Ye tremble. Is it me ye fear?"

He shook his head.

"What, then? Why do ye tremble?"

"I've never stayed in such a fine abode and feel well out of my element." He couldn't meet that smoky gaze, not now when he felt so weak, so vulnerable. "I'll keep my promise and stay in the stables until Mistress Davies passes."

Andras hadn't withdrawn his hand from his shoulder. "Tell me true, Owen, is it me ye fear?"

Ignoring his question, he asked one of his own. "What time of day is it?"

"Midday," Andras answered without pause and stared into his eyes for a long moment.

"Why are the curtains drawn? Why do ye never allow sunlight in?"

"Ye were sleeping, and after a head injury 'tis best to keep the patient calm, the room dark." He removed his hand from his shoulder, reached for a glass of water on the oak table near the bed and handed it to him. "Ye should have an ample amount of liquid if ye are able to stomach it."

"Your hand didn't bleed."

"Pardon?"

"When ye pulled the stopper from the pint of milk, your hand smashed into the jagged glass and tore your skin, yet there was no blood."

He stood back; his gaze locked with his. "Ye are mistaken. I assure ye, the wound bled."

Andras's familiar scent—a virile woodsy aroma—wafted over him, wreaking havoc on his befuddled mind.

"Whatever your overactive imagination has conjured, are ye certain your fear of me doesn't stem from another source?"

Fighting numbing fatigue, Owen struggled to process the question. Duw help him; if the man could read his mind, any answer he offered would be disassembled in a heartbeat. "What other source?" he managed, his pulse launching into an erratic tempo.

Andras's handsome face lost all expression. Owen recognized the man's ability to mask his emotions, a skill he also possessed. "Forgive me. This is not the proper time for this discussion." He ran a hand through the ebony strands at the side of his head and blew air out his lips. "I've prepared a tincture to help ye rest." Pulling a vial from his vest pocket, he popped the stopper with his thumb and handed it to him. "Know this: I'd rather cut off my hand than harm ye."

Owen rose to an elbow and sucked in a short breath. The tremor running through him was so intense the vial shook in his hand. He'd never been important to anyone except his father, never dreamed he'd hear such words from Andras's lips. Fearful his voice would crack under a response he put the bottle to his mouth and downed the bitter liquid. Then he eased his head onto the pillow again, aware of the stitches at the back of his head.

Andras remained at the foot of the bed, his dark form growing blurrier by the minute. The potent remedy warmed Owen's stomach and spread out to his feather-light limbs. His eyes grew heavy and the sound of footsteps heading toward the door came to him through a tunnel.

He surrendered to the blessed world of forgetfulness with Andras's words echoing in his ears, 'I'd rather cut off my hand than harm ye.'

* * *

Owen opened his eyes to ribbons of sunlight dancing across the wooden-plank floor. Remnants of strange dreams surfaced—his body rolling down a steep hill, a dark shape hovering over him, and Andras's reassuring voice. If only he could remember the words from the man's beautiful mouth.

He pushed up in bed and looked about the spacious chamber. He wasn't lying upon his dingy cot in his one-room hut. His cracked, plastered walls weren't adorned with Holbein the Younger's portraits of Edward, Prince of Wales, and Anne of Cleves. Nor did a mahogany wardrobe angled into a corner and matching Edwardian chest at the foot of the four-poster bed fill his vision when he awoke each morn.

A dull ache at the base of his skull took flight. If he'd acquired it tumbling down the steep incline he hadn't been dreaming.

Morsels of conversation trickled into his brain slower than molasses dripping on a wintry day. Heat rose in his cheeks. Had he asked Andras why his wound hadn't bled? Had he questioned the man about the lack of sunlight in the manor? Duw save him, he had.

Perhaps he'd lost all sense of reason at the time, allowed his misguided judgment to speak on his behalf. Warmth enveloped him, the sun's warmth. The curtains weren't drawn shut, and outside, a golden sphere graced a vivid blue sky.

Curiosity compelled him to rise from bed. On wobbly legs, he padded toward the nine-paned window and took in the view of the courtyard below. Carys and a trio of her friends came into view. Perched on a circular stone bench surrounding a fountain, their heads were bowed, their eyes focused on the busy motion of their hands. He wondered what intrigued them so, but then lifted his chin to scan the area for Andras. Disappointment washed over him, and a flicker of recurring doubt. No matter how hard he tried to disavow it, the wound hadn't bled.

The sound of laughter drifted toward the window, drawing his gaze back to the young women. He knew Carys' friends, not personally, but knew of them. If they had an inkling that he, the sin eater, was at this very moment looking down at them from Andras's bedchamber, they'd flee as if a phantom had risen from the grave to chase them down.

Glynnis, daughter of Edward Hale, the village cordwainer, rose from her perch like a graceful swan to show off her wares to Bronwen, old widow Carnes's daughter. In the next instant, Tarren, youngest daughter of Sayer Daw, the stonemason, joined them and motioned for Carys.

Owen stepped back from the window, but not before Carys looked up and offered him a cheery smile. Nine shames! She'd spotted him, and there'd be the devil for her to pay if her companions caught sight of him.

Scurrying toward the bed on bare feet, his big toe caught the polished floor. His arms skittered out, his spine went rigid, and for a moment his upright momentum hung in the balance. After righting himself, he spied his clothing on a nearby chair and walked toward it. He had to get out of the manor, couldn't allow Andras's good name to be dragged through the mud for harboring a sin eater.

He pulled the nightshirt over his head—Andras's, he assumed—and stepped into his trousers. About to push his arms into the sleeves of his shirt, he heard the door creak open.

"And where might ye be off to, Owen Rhys?"

He offered Carys a weak smile. "I'm feeling well now and thought to help Bellamy in the stables."

She put the tray of food down on the night table and adjusted the paisley shawl about her squared shoulders. "I gave my word to Doctor Maddock ye'd not leave this room."

The sound of Andras's name caused his heart to flutter. "I can't stay here, Carys." He put his hands out, palms up. "Ye understand."

"I understand one thing. Ye are not leaving this bed today unless ye have little regard for my wrath." She snuck a peek at his bare chest with narrowed eyes. "I'm not leaving until ye are tucked in snugger than an earwig."

"Aye." His shoulders sagged in defeat. "Turn around and I'll shuck my trousers."

With a smug look, she folded her arms over her chest, showed him her back, and waited.

Owen exchanged the trousers for the nightshirt and climbed beneath the bed covers with his back resting against the headboard. "Ye can look now."

Carys pivoted, walked to the bed and pulled the quilt up to his chin, clucking like a hen as she arranged it. "Now, we'll have no more talk of ye leaving until Andras looks at that lump on your head."

Owen swallowed, hard. Did he want to know the answer to the question nagging him since he'd awakened in the man's bed? Yes, he did. "Where is Doctor Maddock this morning?"

The guarded edge to his voice drew her gaze to his face. "Asleep, as ye should be, and not looking out the window spying on pretty lasses."

Her attempt at humor put him at ease. "I wasn't spying, but I admit to curiosity. What were ye making?"

"Bronwen's mother harvested the last sheaves of corn this morn for dollies." Her features took on a thoughtful expression. "The widow claims spirits live in the fields and die when the corn is scythed. The corn dollies will provide resting places for the spirits and a bountiful harvest will follow next year."

Owen stifled a yawn, then a chuckle, and wondered about her penchant for superstitious musings.

Reaching for the tray next to the bed she set it on

his lap. "I'll leave ye now to Cook's chicken broth and milk." She crossed the room and stopped by the door, turning to him again. "After I have your promise there'll be no more attempts to flee."

The delicious aroma of soup spiraled up his nose and his stomach growled. He wouldn't win the battle with the stubborn Welsh lass in any event. "Ye have my word."

After rewarding him with a smile, Carys closed the door behind her, leaving Owen to stew over a league of unanswered questions about the mysterious physician.

Chapter Three

Owen awoke from dreams of gilded swords, blood-drenched fangs and a commotion at the bedchamber door. Rubbing the sleep from his eyes, he sat up in bed and lit the nearby lantern by the light of a silvery moon. "A missive arrived moments ago." If not for Andras's familiar voice, Owen would have sworn a black-clad phantom crossed the room to hand him the parchment.

He seized the Roman god's gaze for a long, palpable moment before holding the paper against the flickering lamplight:

Come at once. The dead cakes have been prepared. Reese Davies.

Davies's ailing wife had either succumbed or hung on the precipice of death. He grimaced with bitterness. Again he'd don the heavy shroud of a pariah, an outcast in the village, like his father and grandfather—sin eaters one and all. He'd eat the bread, drink the ale, and offer a short prayer at Mistress Davies's deathbed. And like countless times before, he'd consume the sins of the deceased.

Andras stepped from the room while Owen rose from bed and dressed, and thank Duw for it. His feelings for the man had escalated tenfold since arriving at the manor two days ago. The thought of returning to his solitary existence, deprived of gazing upon the visage of his every fantasy, tore at his heart.

In the hallway, Andras handed him a hooded cloak. "'Tis a chilly night; ye will need this."

"I can find Davies's abode on my own."

Andras looked at him askance. "'Tis my duty to pronounce her dead."

"Very well," he said and didn't feel very well at all.

Every minute in the man's presence was more tortuous than the last.

The moon shone full over Abergwaun, lighting the star-strewn path to Davies's opulent country estate. Andras lifted the brass knocker on the massive door and rapped three times. Footsteps reached them from the other side and then the hinges groaned. "Follow me." The servant nodded toward the inlaid marble hallway.

They followed the man's harried steps down a darkened corridor, Owen aware of the distance the brittle-backed valet maintained from the sin eater. Only when death called did the villagers seek him out. Once his duties were concluded, great pains were employed to wipe out all traces of his visit, including burning the mazar bowl his unholy lips had touched.

The stale air in the bedchamber loomed heavy, and there lay Mistress Davies, her long peppered hair fanned out on the crisp, white pillow. Perched in a chair near the bed, her husband alternated between weeping into a linen handkerchief and clasping his wife's bloodless hand.

He watched Andras skirt the bed to stand beside the grieving husband. Leaning over her prone body, the physician checked her pulse before casting Reese a somber gaze. "'Tis time."

"Boy," Reese growled, rising to fetch a tray on the night bureau. "Earn your sixpence." Davies placed a tray upon his wife's abdomen—crusts of bread bearing the woman's name and a bowl of ale. "Nesta's greatest fear was to be relegated to the halls of oblivion. I bid ye take up her sins."

The room fell silent and Owen looked across the bed into the gun-metal depths of Andras's eyes. He'd never tire of the sharp angles and shadowy planes of the man's face. He closed his eyes against the lurid images—the broad shoulders, narrow waist, and powerful legs. Another vision appeared behind his closed eyelids, Andras's heavy sacks and thick sex beneath the snug leather breeches.

Duw forgive me.

It wasn't unusual to hear his father's voice while performing the duties of the sin eater, as he heard it now. 'Andras is under the influence of a gruesome phantom. Be wary, son.'

Vampire or no, Owen had been no less enchanted with the man after hearing the somber words. He'd never seen such a magnificent being, man or woman. The midnight hair enthralled him. The strong, aquiline nose and sculpted features drew him into a tangled labyrinth of cravings he longed to satisfy.

Andras's voice sliced through the deep cavities of his mind. "Owen, there's little time." He stepped up to the bed and lifted a slice of bread from the tray. It was then Mistress Davies's soul escaped through her mouth and drifted toward the open window. Watching the stream of diaphanous, gray smoke, he marveled that he alone bore witness to her essence departing the mortal world. He said a silent prayer the kind, elderly woman would soon meet Duw.

Blowing his nose into the well-worn hankie, the grief-stricken husband interrupted Owen's brief reverie. Clasping the bowl of ale in his hand, Owen downed the liquid and stuffed the bread into his mouth, chewing with care. Closing his eyes, the archaic words tumbled from his lips. "I consume your earthly transgressions, Mistress Davies, and render your sinless soul free. For your peace, I pledge my own soul. Amen."

With a sob, Davies placed a sixpence into Owen's hand and offered a firm nod. His obligation as a sin eater complete, he pulled the hood of his cloak over his long hair, turned, and headed toward the bedchamber door. He'd return home now and do his best to find joy amid his pathetic existence.

Like before, the servant kept his distance while ushering him to the front entry, the sound of their soft footsteps broken by a familiar voice. "Owen, a word with ye before ye journey home."

He turned and gazed into the silver eyes. "'Tis late and the forest is a dangerous place at night."

"Aye, the elders say in the dark of night the woods turn into a realm of the otherworld." He looked away from the beautiful face with a sardonic chuckle. "The elders also have sore elbows from lifting heavy tankards of ale."

Dismissing his humor with a frown, Andras said, "Perhaps ye should sleep in the stables until morn."

The man stood so close, and yet remained untouchable. "Thank ye, sir, but I know the forest well."

"'Tisn't safe, I tell ye; trust me."

Andras looked at him with creased brow as decadent images surfaced. On the cot in his one-room shanty, Andras had mounted him from behind in the same manner the beasts of the woodlands copulated. Did the man hold the power to see what played out in his mind? He had to be gone from this place, couldn't stay in Andras's stable tonight, not after the man had bewitched him so.

His father's voice. *Steer clear of the long tooth, son. Be wary.*

And what if his father's words were true? If Andras was indeed a vampire, did it change his feelings for the man? He wanted him, thirsted for Andras to touch him, stroke his cock, suck his nipples and, yes, thrust deep inside him. Insanity warred with logic, but in the end, sane reason deserted him. He hungered for Andras, long tooth or no.

Owen unclenched his jaw and drew a deep breath.

"Thank ye for your concern, but it goes without saying sin eaters aren't welcome in the village. I'll return to my abode and save ye further duress."

"Very well." Andras's clipped words drew the valet's gaze. "I bid ye a safe journey." With that, Owen turned from the mesmerizing eyes and walked from Davies's estate.

* * *

Moonlight slanted through the pine trees, and in the stillness of the forest, the ocean roared in the distance. Owen stumbled on a rock, regained his footing and followed the silver ribbons down the narrow path.

"The forest holds danger and mystery," his tad always said.

From the inflection in Andras's voice tonight apparently, he felt the same. The man had tried to warn him without alarming the servant. And he'd tried to tell Andras he couldn't spend another night under his roof hungering for his touch.

A fluttering of giant wings to his left brought forth a shocked gasp, and another stumble. He fell to his knees as the moon ducked behind a patch of clouds and pitched his world into darkness. Through the black mystery of the forest, he narrowed his eyes and searched for the airborne creature. When the skin at the nape of his neck prickled, he wished he'd taken Andras's advice and stayed in the stables. The scent of horse dung would have been preferable to the fear anchoring him to the forest floor.

His tad's voice echoed in his ears. "A vampire cannot enter a private dwelling unless the occupant grants him permission. Most long tooth attacks occur outside the abode in isolated areas at night."

Get up, Owen, ye dolt! Run! Ye have got to make it home!

Clambering to his knees, he stilled when a brilliant

flash exploded in the clearing ahead. Beneath a canopy of evergreens, a beast appeared in his line of vision. Nay, it was not a predator of the forest but an upright human form. Shrouded in billowing black, his white skin shone like a beacon under the inky sky. Terror seized him as the phantom advanced at a foot-dragging pace, the undercurrents of death heavy in the morbid air. The ghoul's eyes crazed with bloodlust, his long white fangs descending, he circled him.

Owen's throat constricted with fear, yet the specter's ageless features and hypnotic eyes immobilized him. Time ceased to exist and his immortality rushed forward. Death clung to his pores; he felt it surround him like a black shroud.

Lladd amser. His father's words for Killing Time lashed about him like a hard rain. He knew someone would die again soon, but never suspected the someone would be him.

In the breath of a heartbeat, a new shape burst onto the scene, exploding through the bracken with lightning speed. Without pause, the newcomer lunged, the flash of his sword powerful and true. Metal met metal in a timeless dance of deflect and parry, to meet time and again beneath the shadowy moon.

A peal of laughter bounced off the trees. "Well done, Andras. Someone has taught ye well."

His name fell from Owen's lips on a whisper. "Andras?"

The scene played out before him like an act from a Shakespearean play...except the characters knew one another.

Andras gave no answer to his enemy's false compliment, but rather countered with a vicious upward slice toward his groin. The being lunged with a heavy thrust and sliced open Andras's shoulder. Owen focused on the torn fabric of his jerkin, waited for a stream of blood to arc through the vaporous air, and groaned when it failed to appear.

Vampire against vampire, their bodies whirled and twisted in a maelstrom of flesh and bone. They thrashed and tumbled on the ground only to continue the fight moments later in the branches of a massive oak.

Paralyzed, Owen watched with his heart in his throat.

Long fangs gnashed and an anonymous bloodcurdling scream rent the air. Still it didn't end. Blades clanked beneath moonbeams and then Andras pirouetted with the agility of a jungle cat. Time ceased to exist as he brought the claymore up high above his head. On the downswing, the mighty blade keened its death knell and severed the long tooth's head from his neck. The demon's limp body tumbled from the branch and landed three feet from Owen. Gray smoke rolled from the creature's open cavity, his body recoiling like a giant serpent's tail in the last throes of death.

Owen clutched his abdomen and retched. Long seconds later and fighting off waves of dizziness, he lifted his head and stared into the ghost-white face of Andras Maddock. Bent at the waist, the physician gasped for precious air, yet kept his keen sight on the periphery of the clearing.

Owen followed his gaze with sickening dread. Were other long tooths waiting to attack? And who or what was Andras?

Andras jumped from a low branch of the tree with the sinuous grace of a cat. He holstered his sword in the scabbard about his waist. "Can ye walk?"

Owen nodded.

"I suggest we leave. Now."

"But, who—?"

"If we remain here, more will come, and I cannot fight them all."

"More?"

Andras straightened and studied him with narrowed perception. "'Tis certain."

He fought through the rising panic and looked at Andras's shoulder. "No blood again."

"Aye, but 'tis the least of our worries. I'll explain soon if we live long enough."

Mesmerized by the voice and in shock over the scene that had played out before him, Owen looked into the cold, lifeless eyes of the dead man. "Vampires here in Pembrokeshire?"

"I could ask the same: a sin eater in our midst?"

Owen knelt beside what remained of the long tooth and tried to form the words he knew by heart. His lips moved, but no sound came forth.

Andras shouted his alarm. "What in the hell do ye think ye are doing?"

"Claiming his sins."

"Are ye daft? Traherne is a pure-blood bequeathed with mystical powers. He suffered none of the typical weaknesses known to his kind."

"I'm a sin eater, Andras."

"Ye mustn't assume his transgressions."

"I've learned to divest myself of the sins I assume."

Andras's mocking laughter echoed around him. "Not from the oldest vampire in the universe. If ye think to regurgitate his sins ye are mistaken." He shook his head. "Ye could die."

"Pity, that."

"What's that supposed to mean?"

"It can't kill me." Owen placed his hand over his heart. "I'm already dead."

Compassion flitted through Andras's eyes, replaced by steeled determination. "Get off your knees; recant whatever portion of the creed entered your mind. Do it now, before—"

Demons howled in the distance, clotting Owen's blood.

Andras looked above the tree tops. "They come."

Before Owen could react, Andras flung him onto his back, soared into the night sky and flew above the trees.

Another wave of dizziness washed over Owen, whether from the towering heights or the fact he clung to the neck of a vampire, he didn't know. He fought back the bile in his throat and closed his eyes, relieved that within minutes they landed in front of his humble abode. Scrambling from Andras's back, he collapsed to the ground in a heap, and clutched the hard-packed earth.

A hand reached out to him. "Rise now, we must get inside."

"Is it true what my tad said . . . a long tooth will not enter unless invited?" "'Tis true," Andras said with a half-smile.

Owen hobbled to the entrance, kicked it open with the toe of his boot and nodded for Andras to follow him. He crossed himself, barricaded the door with a chest, and turned to stare into the face of the most handsome vampire he'd ever laid eyes on.

Chapter Four

Andras watched Owen stagger toward the hearth and return to the cot with a pan of warm water and a clean cloth. "Allow me to cleanse your wounds."

"I'm the physician," he replied with a sardonic chuckle. "I assure ye; my wounds will heal without fuss."

Andras scanned the one-room shelter. A crude portrait of a middle-aged woman, another of a fly-cart drawn by a sway-backed horse, and a cross made from wheat stalks adorned the walls.

"The cross belonged to my mother." Owen said following his gaze.

"The woman in the portrait?"

"In her younger days, painted by a villager with a keen eye." Owen set the bowl down on a crude table and seemed to have difficulty meeting his eyes. "Will ye remove the jerkin and shirt and allow me look at the shoulder wound?"

Andras shrugged. "Ye doubt my word? Very well." He removed the clothing and watched Owen's eyes widen.

"'Tis as ye said. No blood and little injury to speak of now." Green eyes scanned his bare chest before Owen reached out and touched his warm flesh. "The wound has healed as if the breath of God whispered over it."

"Not God. Diawl perhaps."

"No, ye are a kind man, Andras, not one marked by the devil."

"At one time, perhaps, before Traherne found me in the woods."

Owen licked his bottom lip and looked into his eyes, the pungent aroma of sweat and heat engulfing them. "Is that how it happened. . . Traherne turned ye?"

Andras nodded, aware of the unfathomable allure filling the empty space between them. For too many years he'd watched Owen, waiting, hoping one day the sin eater's son would recognize the enigmatic magnetism. Everything about the young man mystified him—the deep, chestnut hair falling in a wild tumble about his shoulders, the deep green eyes that shone like precious stones, mostly his gentle, unassuming nature. God, how he'd tried to dispel the feelings, more so after the night Traherne set upon him in the forest. How many times in the last five years had he laughed over the perverse irony? Under normal circumstances, the odds of Owen sharing his same carnal desires were nonexistent, but him loving a vampire, out of the question.

"He allowed ye to live?"

"Accidental." Andras struggled to dispel the gruesome visions. "He thought I'd bleed out on the forest floor and that would be the end of his dilemma."

Owen released a long, audible breath.

"Your eyes hold many questions."

"Aye, too many to notch on the trunk of a wide-girthed yew."

Entranced by his presence, Andras found himself studying the angular planes of his face. "Ask, and I'll do my best to appease your curiosity."

"What is your age?"

He smiled. "Are ye not the same as Carys, twenty-five summers?"

"It must be true, for twenty-one summers passed before my tad died four years ago."

"And are ye good with numbers?"

He nodded. "Fair."

"Carys was ten summers when her parents passed and I was twenty summers when I took her in."

"Thirty-five," he said with a smile. "Ten years my

senior."

"Correct, now what else do ye wish to know?"

"What brought ye to the shire?"

"Ah, when I finished my schooling, I had a desire to ply my trade near the sea. Wdig and the neighboring village of Abergwaun seemed the logical choice. They had great need of a physician and I had great need to serve."

"Carys accompanied ye?"

"The choice was hers. She could have remained at Sycharth Castle in north Wales, my childhood home, but finds my foppish, eccentric Uncle Maxen a wee overbearing."

Owen took a quick intake of breath. "One of the noblest houses in all of Wales?"

"At one time, aye, but few know of my origins and I prefer it to remain thus."

His eyes darkened with pain. "Who would converse with a sin eater?"

"Me," he replied wishing he could erase the defeat in Owen's voice.

Andras's heart took a perilous leap when the emerald lights of his eyes shifted. "Why do I feel this powerful connection between us?"

He knew the question would arise one day, and a thousand times he'd rehearsed his counter. Now the inopportune time was at hand and he struggled to find the words. "Are ye certain ye wish to hear the answer?"

Owen nodded but held his ragged breath.

"I knew your father."

"Everyone knew of my father, but few acknowledged him. Unless they required him to draw out the vestiges of evil from a loved one's soul, free the corpse of its attachments to earth so it might enter the Kingdom of Heaven."

"Sin eaters deal with the living too. Did your father

not teach ye souls can be damaged in different ways?"

"Aye," Owen said. "My father said no matter what others do to us, there's a proper way to behave to preserve our morality."

"Yes and your father spoke of other things—that humans are often victims of shameful acts and carry guilt which is not theirs to bear. It's this burden of guilt and shame of the event that causes wounds to the soul."

Closing his eyes, Owen looked at the floor. "I grow weary of wearing the heavy yoke of a sin eater; long to believe there's more to life than the legacy left by those who went before me."

Turbulent emotions gripped Andras. The need to hold Owen in his arms, to comfort him, refused to die. "Is it not true the sin eater saves the dying from Hell, but also ensures they won't roam the earth as apparitions? Do they not perform a service for the living as well?"

"Yes," Owen whispered. "But ye didn't answer my question. How do ye know what my father spoke of? In what way did ye know him?"

"After I was attacked by Traherne and left to die in the forest, the sin eater found me."

"My tad?"

"Aye."

Through the window, the soft rustle of trees penetrated the stillness. A fresh wave of desire coursed through Andras. The dull ache of need he'd lived with so long whipped around him like a lash until he couldn't breathe. Once he told Owen the entire truth, what would he think? Would he believe his vigilance, nay, his obsession, to protect him from all things was nothing more than duty, a sacred oath to a dying man?

He stepped into his answer with care. "He could have finished me off, perhaps should have. A merciful man, your father."

"He took your sins as his own?"

"My mortal sins, and then he saved me, knowing I would rise a vampire." Andras drew an exasperated breath, preparing for the rest of his confession. "He bartered for my immortal life with two stipulations."

Owen blew air through his lips. "Tell me."

"I vowed to never drink the blood of humans and gave my oath to watch over ye when he passed."

Hurt masked his eyes, but not fear. "Because of your vow to my father, ye have now become a vampire hunter and the keeper of his son?"

"Nay, neither." Andras cupped his chin and forced him to meet his eyes. "I'm not a vampire slayer, but a physician."

"But ye killed Traherne?"

"Aye, he left me no choice. I gave my word I'd watch out for ye, and have kept my oath to your father."

Owen bolted from the chair, tipping it over in the process. "Leave. I don't want to hear the rest."

"Ye must hear me out." He rose from the cot and reached Owen in less time than it took him to pull the latch. Andras spun him around, pinning him against the door, their bodies separated by their clothing. Duw help him, the world spun and his body hummed like a lightning fork. "I've watched ye from afar, held ye here." He placed a hand over his heart.

"Because of a vow ye made to my father!"

"Nay." Andras shook his head and drowned in the wet, moss-green eyes. "Despite the vow, I've cared; have watched ye stumble through the pain of loneliness and despair." Owen's heart thrummed a mad tempo against his chest, and raw, primal need washed over him. *Not now, not like this.* "Owen, ye don't have to remain a sin eater."

Anger came sudden. "Ye are not the only one who swore an oath to my sire!" He snorted. "Born a sin eater, I'm unsavory, destined to lead an afterlife in Hell carrying the sins of others. Visions of death haunt me night and day"

"Speak. What kind of visions?"

"Muddied prophecies. I don't know who, only that death stalks Pembrokeshire."

"'Tis not too late for ye to walk away from here, leave."

"Aye, 'tis too late," he whispered. "'Twas the day ye arrived in Abergwaun."

He shouldn't have spoken the words. Andras's resolve faded like stars in the morning sky. Owen's face swam before him, paler than usual because of what he'd witnessed this night. His eyes searched his face as though looking at it for the last time. Scents mingled: the damp earth, a scant aroma of wild herbs, and restrained desire.

Beneath the candle's sputtering flame, Andras saw the pulse beat in the hollow of his throat. Owen's hand slid up his arm; stopping near the ridge of the wound he'd earned fighting Traherne.

The unsteady gasp of Owen's breath fanned his lips. So close now he couldn't have turned away if a tidal wave capsized the meager abode. A force more powerful than Duw's thunder heaved between them, and then it was too late for Andras to stop.

Owen's touch on his arm, the taste of his lips melding with his, sent a jolt of unbearable pleasure rushing through him. The sin eater's fingers wound their way into the hair at the back of his neck and Owen drew him deeper into the kiss. Andras parted his lips with his tongue, evoking a breathless moan and a defenseless surrender of his body against Owen's.

His manhood swelled and ached, the surge of blood rushing to the head almost unbearable. Duw help him. If Owen took it in his mind right now to seek out the hard shaft, Andras's release would burst forth the instant he touched him.

The kiss deepened, Owen converging on him like a starved beast, his mouth devouring his, his tongue giving back what it took. There was nothing in the world except Owen, no brutal visions, no vampires. He tasted like summer rain and Andras couldn't slake his thirst fast enough.

He longed to feel his hot skin against Owen's, pull from his lips another moan and another, but it couldn't happen. Owen's all-consuming vulnerability frightened him, and oaths, dying wishes and resultant repercussions flooded his senses.

Andras broke from the kiss and stepped back, his breaths coming hard.

"No," Owen said, still writhing against him, his hands clinging to his shoulders.

"We mustn't, not like this." He reached up and removed his hands. "We are entering very dangerous water here, and I feel ye—"

"Do not feel, do not think. It's what I've wanted for so long."

"Ye are lonely, vulnerable. It would be a grave mistake to take advantage of ye without allowing ye time to think of all we've talked about, digest everything that happened this night."

His eyes were shut, his breathing erratic. "Traherne turning ye doesn't change my feelings for ye. I don't care about any of that."

"I care, Owen. We don't know what will happen now. Above all, I must keep ye safe. If Dagan thinks to get to me through ye, he'll not hesitate to act upon it."

Owen opened his eyes. "Dagan? Who is this ye speak of?"

"Traherne's son. He'll come to satisfy his lust for revenge."

"And ye will fight him?"

"Them, Dagan and his followers." The aching tenderness of Owen's kiss remained on his lips, making it hard for him to think. "I'll do whatever is necessary to protect the villagers...and ye."

"How many followers?"

"I don't know, perhaps a handful."

"One against so many? Ye'll die!"

"Ye can't know that."

"I know this. My father said a long tooth's powers are measured by his years. Tell me he was wrong."

"He spoke the truth."

"Ye said Traherne was the oldest vampire in the universe and so his son must also be old, but ye have five years as...."

"Monster, demon, nesuferitul. Why don't ye name me for what I am?"

"Let me help ye, Andras. Make me like ye and I'll fight by your side."

He placed a finger over Owen's lips. "Don't ever speak to me of this again. I took an oath to save lives, not take them."

"I want to be like ye." He whispered the words as though the pain of the world resided in his voice. "I want to be...with ye."

Andras shook his head. "There are things ye don't know of."

"Tell me, help me understand."

"Although Traherne turned me, I won't become wholly vampiric unless I feed on another human. Heed me well, Owen. Have ye any idea how I struggle with these bestial cravings, long to sate my lust on blood, a human's blood." He narrowed his eyes and drew the words out. "Your blood."

"Forgive me, I had no idea."

"'Tis the one thing I have left, a shred of my former

self. A curse of the worst kind—undead and yet not living, walking in darkness and longing for daylight." He walked to the cot, plucked his shirt and jerkin from the mattress and dressed.

"Where are ye going?"

Andras looked through the window. "I must leave now." He nodded toward the pale light of morning. "Don't fear, the long tooths will not return this day."

"That's not what I fear," Owen said his voice shaky. "I fear ye will not return."

The sexy mouth smiled, and the deep silver eyes shone like moonlight. "That fear is unfounded."

His cherished words split the quiet confines of the cottage and then the vampire fled through the door as silent as a thief in the night.

Chapter Five

Dagan's journey from Romania wasn't without incident. His clan had been thirsty en route, ravenous for blood, necessitating several stops in secluded villages to feast. Appeasing their mischievous appetite had also waylaid them for a spell. Near Pembroke Castle, Estevan discovered a plot of werewolf graves and wasted little time in alerting the others. Several hours were lost desecrating the lycans' eternal resting places, and another two covering their scent after the despoiling.

Now that they'd arrived at their destination in Wales, Dagan walked the confines of the northwest tower in Carew Castle and thought about the many times he'd visited the once magnificent structure over the centuries.

He closed his eyes and drew forth the energy in the room. Did the Lord and his pet monkey that had died in the tower a century ago still lurk among its ruins? No, the essences of their misguided spirits failed to appear. Apparently, they'd abandoned their posts like the other prior occupants.

Since he had an affinity for gloom and shadows, Dagan's surroundings met his every expectation, but wouldn't suit his father. With that in mind, he conjured an ebony throne with gilded arms, scattered the rodents to the four winds and called forth yards of billowing red silk to adorn the walls. Ah, yes, he must do something about the dirt and foliage rising up from the decrepit brick floor. Calling forth the finest marble from Italy, moments later an inlaid floor, reminiscent of the sculptures from the Parthenon, lay beneath his feet.

He walked to the throne, eased into the cushioned seat and wondered why his clan hadn't returned with his father yet. The same sinister foreboding that had followed him from Romania settled in. It wasn't like Traherne to be late for a rendezvous, thus the reason he'd ordered his relations to scour the countryside until they located him. Something was amiss, and yet even in all his infinite wisdom, the symbols and images of the conundrum eluded him.

Dagan smiled. Once they had the Prince of Wales's sword in their possession, their strength would increase tenfold. The clans would no longer be relegated to the night world; the sword would grant them immunity from the sun's harsh rays. Fighting his liege Lord for the sword was another matter. He couldn't think about that now; he would obtain the sword and deal with the scaly abomination later.

Overcome with exhilaration, he clapped his hands. It seemed fitting that his father, the oldest vampire in the universe, would rule the one sect in the world that could walk in daylight.

Perhaps his sire had already obtained the sword and meant to surprise him this very night. Dagan put his head back, closed his eyes and reminded himself that all great things were worth waiting for.

* * *

Jolted from his trance-like state, Dagan jackknifed up.

Before his ebony throne stood his uncle, Estevan, with the grisly corpse of his father draped across his arms. "Found him in the woods after...."

Revenge beat a savage tattoo in Dagan's chest and escaped his lips in a bestial yowl. He looked beyond Estevan's bowed head and focused on the anxious faces of his father's kin—Alvaro, his brother-in-law; Kale, his nephew; and Emmett and Johan, his sire's cousins.

After rising from his perch, the heavy fall of his footsteps echoed against the marble floor. He looked down at his father's headless body and closed his eyes against the debilitating pain. "I pray ye brought his entire remains?"

Alvaro cleared his throat drawing Dagan's gaze to the coarse gunnysack in his outstretched hand. "Here, my Lord."

"He leaves the castle to finish the job he started five years ago and returns thus?"

Kale's reverent tone reached him. "Andras couldn't have slain him without the sword, my Lord."

"Gods be damned, the cursed weapon will be the death of us all!"

"It possesses magick," Estevan whispered. "Has served Maddock's predecessors well for centuries."

Enraged, Dagan tipped his head back and felt the veins in his neck bulge. "I swear your death will be avenged, my father!" With harried stride, he returned to his throne and struggled to control his wrath. "No more, do ye hear?" He looked at those who had served his father well, and would now serve him, his gaze settling on Emmett and next Johan. "Ye will track his every move and report back to me. If Maddock leaves his manor at sunset, follow him until he reaches his destination. Find out who calls upon him and from whence they came."

Johan shrugged. "The healer's visitors are many, my Lord."

"Then slake your thirst and reduce their numbers."

Emmett exchanged a malevolent sneer with Johan. "The sword, my Lord? Should we search his residence and deliver it to ye?"

Dagan's laughter ricocheted off the domed ceiling. "Ye fool. Do ye think to succeed where the greatest vampire on earth failed?"

"I meant no disrespect, my Lord."

Dagan tapped the arms of his throne with pale,

white fingers. "Rest assured; the rapier will be in my possession before I leave this godforsaken land."

"Forgive me, my brave leader, but if your father failed in his endeavor to kill Maddock and retrieve the Prince of Wales's claymore...."

He rose and looked down on them from the dais. "Every being, man or creature, is possessed of weakness. Find Maddock's and I'll have him on bended knee bartering for the life of his loved one in exchange for the sword."

Kale's eyes narrowed. "He's not sought the path of the vampire after Traherne turned him. Your father said he continues his practice as a healer, albeit in altered form." He snorted through a chuckle. "At one time, Maddock clung to dreams of mortal love, but your sire robbed him of such foolish notions."

Estevan looked down at the broken body in his arms and grimaced. "The fine people of Abergwaun wouldn't cavort with one of the insufferable."

"True, but he planned to share his life with someone before my father found him in the woods. One must believe Maddock has yielded to his cravings and transformed his beloved." A sinister laugh spewed from his throat. "His thirst for blood is as strong as ours."

"Yes, my Lord," Kale said.

Dismissing them with a wave of his hand, Dagan slumped onto the throne again. "Well, what are ye waiting for? Ye have your orders."

Estevan snuck a sheepish glance from behind a veil of long, white hair. "What shall I do with your father?"

Fighting back anguish, Dagan closed his eyes. "Return him to his crypt. When our business is concluded here, we'll hold a service befitting the greatest undead that ever walked the Underworld."

Estevan bowed at the waist. "As ye wish."

"Return posthaste, ye are needed here."

"Yes, my Lord."

"Kale, take up a post near the gatehouse. We can't afford to underestimate Maddock's cunning."

"Alone, Dagan?" Kale's brow furrowed.

"Do ye require an army to assist in this endeavor?"

"I fear the werewolves will rise from the graves we desecrated near Pembroke Castle."

"'Tis fallacy werewolves can rise from the dead. What's more, they don't have the ability to follow our scent now that we covered it." Dagan pinned him with a lethal glare. "Ye have more to fear from Maddock and the Prince of Wales's claymore than ye do werewolves. Now do what I ask and don't leave the barbican unless I send for ye."

Dagan's minions turned on their heels and walked from the hall. He watched their retreating backs and then lifted his head skyward. "On my sacred oath, I'll cut out his heart and place it in your still hands."

* * *

Andras flung himself into a chair in his study and cupped his chin in his hand. He couldn't stop thinking about Owen and the inexplicable draw between them. He shouldn't have caved in to his lust, his all-consuming yearning for the one person who righted his world by his mere presence.

No good could ever come of it. His life as he once knew it was gone, snuffed out like a candle thanks to Traherne and his godforsaken quest to obtain the sword of his ancestors. Passed down in his family for centuries, he knew of the mysticism surrounding the weapon, but never thought to test the hypothesis until the black hand of fate entered his life. And test it he did. When he discovered he could walk in sunlight while holstering the sword, he never questioned the weapon's power again.

He'd gone to the only person he could trust, Bellamy, his blade smith. The man had met his confession without pause or recrimination, and had convinced him to take up the weapon and defend himself against the dark lords of the otherworld. After endless weeks of tutelage and tortuous lessons, Bellamy had taught him to thrust and parry with consummate skill.

His great-grandfather many times removed, Owain ap Gruffydd Fychan, had led the men of west Wales in liberating the proud Welsh from the bondage of their English enemies. The weapon had served his progenitor well, as it would him now in defeating the bloodsucking undead.

Other than Bellamy, and now Owen, only one other person knew of his decent into Hell— Carys—the lass he'd raised after her parents were slain. He trusted her beyond measure, loved her as his own, and she'd returned that love one hundred times over.

Andras walked to the window and pulled back the heavy curtains. The sun had dropped beyond the horizon an hour ago, affording him a few precious hours of freedom. Never again would the brilliant rays warm his flesh, gone forever were the days of walking his beloved moors in daylight and inhaling the intoxicating scent of rain-kissed heather— unless he carried the sword on his person. Traherne had robbed him of all things he once held close to his heart...customary rituals he took for granted.

Bitterness rose like bile in his throat, sweetened by the thought Traherne would never again hold the power to deliver another into the realm of Hell. Others would come now, as he knew they would when he'd cleaved the vampire's head from his body. He had no choice. He'd surrender his life, everything he ever was or hoped to be to ensure that Owen wouldn't suffer the same fate.

The sin eater had solidified his suspicions, prophesied that death would come to the shire...many deaths. The perverse irony, that he, a physician, had been transformed into a vampire and could do little now to uphold his oath, choked him.

A frantic knock at the door jolted him from his bleak thoughts. "Enter."

Carys' ashen face rose before him. "Andras, ye must come; something terrible has happened to Glynnis."

"Glynnis Hale?"

"Aye. She didn't return home last evening. After scouring the countryside, her father found her in an abandoned manor in lower town. He makes his way here now carrying her in his arms."

The villagers had gathered in swarms by the time Andras met them outside Maddock Manor. Through the parted crowd, Edward Hale walked forward, his daughter's limp body stretched across his thick arms.

"Ye must save her, 'tis not too late," he keened above the shocked onlookers.

After one look at the pallid color of her skin and the deep wound in her neck, Andras knew the girl was beyond saving; she had died hours ago. With harried steps he closed the short distance between them and took Glynnis from her father's embrace. Then he shook his head. "She's gone."

The girl's mother collapsed to the ground, her high-pitched keens slicing through the cool night air. The angst-stricken father clasped his hands to the sides of his head and rocked back on his heels as if to wish the world away.

A voice from the crowd rose above the chaos. "A beast set upon her."

"'Tis a monster in our midst!" another roared.

Edward leaned over his daughter's corpse and

brushed a finger over her pale cheek. "What are we to do, Andras? My child has been murdered, taken away long before her due."

Andras's perceptive gaze lingered on the puncture wounds at the side of her neck and a chill shivered down his spine. He lifted his head and scanned the distant terrain with the acute awareness Traherne's sect had announced their arrival in Abergwaun. Did Glynnis's death stem from a lone act of bloodlust or did Dagan mean to draw him out? How many did they number and would the killings continue until they'd satisfied their revenge? Or did Dagan now covet the sword as his father had? A sickening dread crawled through his gut.

The village clogger raised his knife in the air. "'Twas the sin eater, I tell ye."

"Aye, Glynnis said he watched her from yonder window." Edward pointed to the second story of Maddock Manor.

"Oh no, 'tis not true." Carys's tear-stained face appealed to the frenzied masses. "Owen is a gentle soul; he would not harm a hair on her head."

"Do ye deny ye harbored the sin eater in the manor?" Mrs. Hale's accusatory tone chilled the blood in Andras's veins. "Enamored of my daughter's beauty, he stalked the lass and set upon her while she picked berries."

A chorus of jeers split the night.

"I beseech ye to remain calm." Andras pleaded. "Allow the authorities to investigate.

Carys speaks the truth; Owen Rhys isn't capable of such a crime."

"He's possessed of sin, the most unholy of all mankind," Mistress Hale interjected. "Not until he showed his face in Abergwaun did one of our own die."

Paranoia and suspicion laced the air as Andras

addressed them. "We don't know at this juncture what took her life. Allow me to examine her and I'll make a full report to the authorities." He tried to make his voice sound indifferent while inside waves of alarm rolled through him. He'd seen unruly crowds before; he knew they were capable of acting like a pack of rabid hounds when riled. He called on a reserve of fortitude and turned to the girl's father with feigned composure. "Please, Edward, allow me to examine Glynnis and I'll get to the bottom of it." He faced the crowd. "Go home, embrace your children, and thank the Almighty they're safe this night."

Disgruntled and muttering under their breaths, they dispersed and headed toward the steep incline that would deliver them to lower town.

Andras looked into the moist eyes of Glynnis's father. "Will ye trust me to see to your daughter? I'll treat her with the utmost care."

Edward wiped the dribble from his nose with his sleeve. "Will ye light candles? She's fearful of the dark."

Andras nodded. "Go now, take your wife home and I'll call on ye in the morning." He waited until the crowd disappeared down the knoll before turning to Carys.

The terror in her eyes mirrored his when she looked at the wounds in Glynnis's slender neck. "Oh, Andras, the long tooths have returned?"

His heart heavy, he nodded.

"But why, what do they seek?"

"That which they sought before, the Prince's sword." He paused, weighing his words. How could he tell Carys he'd killed Traherne in order to save Owen? He trusted her with his life, and she him. In the end, he decided to tell her. "The night Owen took on the sins of Mistress Davies, he was set upon in the woods."

She gasped.

"I followed him and a fight ensued."

Carys crossed herself and stared at him with questioning eyes.

"I killed the most powerful long tooth in the universe with the Prince's sword."

"Duw save us! What are we to do?"

"His family comes now to avenge his death and take possession of the weapon."

Another gasp. "Ye must go to Owen, tell him about Glynnis. There's no telling what the riotous villagers will do come morn if they suspect the sin eater."

Obliged to heed Carys's request yet compelled to stay away from Owen, Andras battled with warring emotions. A tangible bond existed between him and the sin eater, had from the moment he first looked at Owen after he'd arrived in Pembrokeshire. Deeper than the river Wye and stronger than the chains of Hell, he could no longer fight against it.

Before Traherne turned him, a minute spark of hope existed that one day, Owen might return that love. Surely, he felt the same intense physical awareness whenever their eyes met. Andras would take him away from this life of hopelessness to a place where no one would know about his past. For a brief moment, his heart sang and then despair threatened to bring him to his knees. He was a long tooth for Christ's sake, a bloodsucking predator, and he'd be damned if he'd deliver Owen to a doomed life of failure ten times worse than what he lived now.

"Andras?"

"Yes, Carys, I heard ye."

"I'll stay with Glynnis until ye return. Come," she said hooking her arm in his to lead him back to the manor.

Andras laid Glynnis down on the table in his laboratory and covered her with a sheet. Poor unsuspecting lass. Her only mistake was being in the wrong place at the right time when Traherne's demons came across her.

He closed his eyes against the montage of images rushing forth—Traherne circling him before lunging for his throat, the innate rush of euphoria that had washed over him as the vampire drained the blood from his veins, and the debilitating pain as he lay on the forest floor gasping for breath.

He turned to Carys. "Ye mustn't let anyone enter the manor while I'm gone."

Her brow furrowed. "What if someone becomes ill and needs your attention?"

"Ye must listen to me now, Carys! No one will come while I'm gone, and if they do, under no circumstances are ye to ask them into the manor."

Her eyes pooled with tears. "Very well."

"Long tooths have the ability to mimic any human or animal form. Traherne first approached me in the woods in the likeness of a doe." He ran his hands over a day's stubble on his chin. "I apologize for raising my voice."

"Apology accepted," she said.

"Vampires, in any form, can't enter a residence unless they're invited by a person who resides there, so let us come up with a secret passage."

Her head came up and she smiled. "What shall it be?"

He smiled in return. "Ye choose."

Despite the grave situation, a giggle left her lips. "Tatws-a-llaeth."

"Potatoes and buttermilk? 'Tis a fine choice; no one would suspect such a secret passage."

"Be careful, Andras. I'm so frightened."

"Don't be frightened." He walked over to her and placed his hand on the silken locks at the crown of her head. "I'll not let anything happen to ye. Bellamy will be in the stables until I return. If ye need anything, call out for him."

"Aye. Go now, and may Duw travel with ye."

Outside, Andras took to the sky and headed south. Toward Wdig and toward Owen, the sin eater.

Chapter Six

An innate sense of curiosity drew Owen to the hearth, and to the nearby wooden crate. After his father passed, he'd relegated the man's meager possessions and his collection of cherished books to the trunk and hadn't looked at the contents since. If memory served him, he'd find not only several volumes on Welsh history, but another on legend and lore of Wales.

He removed the lid from the crate and sorted through the books until he found what he searched for, *Demons and Other Mystical Creatures of Wales.* Thumbing through the pages quickly, he found the chapter entitled Lords of the Underworld: Vampyres.

He swallowed the lump in his throat and scanned the page, his eyes settling on a passage in the middle: *The vampyre is the most dreaded and feared creature of the supernatural world. He's not only obtained immortality, but has the ability to alter his appearance, fly through the night sky, and traverse the ground under the guise of the wolf or a wisp of smoke. After seducing his victims through hypnotic measures or mind control, the vampyre will drain them of their blood thereby bolstering his strength and power. A vampyre might possess beauty beyond one's imagination or be hideously marked.*

Owen's heart launched into a triple beat and a fine bead of sweat broke out on his forehead. *The mouth is thought to be the way the soul leaves the body, and also the way evil spirits are allowed to enter. If one has slain a vampyre in Wales, it is advised the mouth be stuffed with a consecrated object or stitched shut and sprinkled with holy water.*

Owen turned the page with an acute sense of trepidation and read his third and final passage: *Spiritual vampyres draw the life energy from their victims and at times, their very souls. This species of vampyre does not merely feed on blood but the victim's essence in order to survive.*

He slammed the book shut, tossed it back into the crate and replaced the lid. Then he rose and paced the cottage, the words from the tome tumbling through his head. He didn't need to read the passages to know Andras was a vampire; the man had admitted it. What he wouldn't give to have known Andras before he arrived in Pembrokeshire. Had he always possessed such unearthly beauty or had he accrued it since Traherne turned him?

And what species of long tooth was Traherne? Had he not only fed on Andras's blood, but sucked the very soul from the man? Andras, soulless? Nay, it could not be. He'd witnessed innumerable acts of compassion from the man while ministering to the sick, watched his eyes flood with empathy when they passed into the other world.

His intestines wound into a reef knot. Had Andras played him false with his words of coveting him from afar and holding a place for him in his heart? Were those the words of a demon possessed of hypnotic capabilities or the words of a man who cared deeply? The questions festered and churned until Owen knew only one thing: Andras was a very dark and very beautiful vampire.

He plucked his fiddle from the case and bolted outside, the questions rattling his brain until he could no longer think. Settling into a rocking chair on the stoop, he drew a deep breath and gazed at the cloud-hung peaks of the mountains in the distance.

Hopelessness cloaked him. He had little in the way of earthly possessions—his goats, a roof over his head and his fiddle—tangible objects that could be taken away in the blink of an eye. But the two things he possessed that no one could ever take from him were his good name and his love of the song.

His father's words from long ago found him, '*Enw da yw'r trysor gorau*' a good name is the best of treasures. No matter what the villagers thought of him—of all sin eaters—he had his good name and had done nothing to dishonor it.

Plucking the fiddle from his knees, he tucked it under his chin, and with his arm stretched out, rested the beloved cwth on his collarbone. He angled the bow across the strings and strummed out a repertoire of ancient Welsh tunes his father had taught him. Losing track of time while playing, he cast aside melancholy thoughts of vampires, sin eaters and the quandaries plaguing him. Whisked away in the poignant, artful blending of tunes reminiscent of his Celtic roots, he didn't see the dark shape watching him from a cluster of yews several feet away until he placed the fiddle at his feet.

Andras.

He shuddered, as much from the eloquent dark visage as from the memory of his kiss.

Despite the passages in the book and the questions afflicting him, one thing remained clear. He wanted Andras, ached with the desire to touch him. He saw only the magnificent features, the hard, powerful body—a well-oiled apparatus—as the man advanced.

Advanced? Duw help me.

The intoxicating musk of the man's skin drifted over him and still Andras didn't speak. The implication of his hypnotic gaze stoked the fire raging in Owen's gut. The words from the book echoed in his ears: *After seducing his victim with his hypnotic eyes, the vampyre will drain him of blood.* Even knowing this, he couldn't tear his gaze away from Andras's beauty.

In a blur of motion, onward he came, his

mesmerizing eyes blazing luminous red. With an unexplainable momentum, Andras transported them into the cottage and slammed the door behind them. Pressed up against the wall, his senses dazzled, Owen lifted his eyes and met the silver orbs he'd visited so many times in his dreams. "Did ye know I played the fiddle?" Gaw, what a dimwitted question to ask while in Andras's possessive embrace. Have ye lost your senses, Owen?

The somnolent lilt to Andras's arrogant voice sent fire racing through his bloodstream. "Yes. Did I not tell ye I've watched ye from afar?" Without waiting for him to answer he added, "Does it frighten ye to know a vampire has longed to look upon your face whenever possible; would risk everything for one stolen glance to feel the lightning coursing through him that only Duw can call forth?"

Owen's heart shattered. He buried his hands in Andras's thick hair and pulled him down into the kiss he craved, would die for. He didn't really want to know the answer; not now. Not when Andras was here in the flesh, allowing him to touch him, stirring something deep inside him he'd only wondered about.

With his hand locked against his spine, Andras pulled him closer and devoured his lips, sweeping his tongue through every crevice as if to memorize the taste of him. Borne of need and unrequited love the kiss deepened, became almost brutal in its intensity. Of its own volition, Owen's primitive moan of need filled Andras's mouth.

Andras's flesh trembled beneath his exploring fingers. What would happen if he dropped his hand and slid it across his body to where his heavy flesh dwelt? The urge to do so crushed him. What if the opportunity never came again in his lifetime? His sex throbbed and again, an agonizing fire rose from his groin and spread to every limb.

He shut his eyes, slid his hand down and clasped Andras's engorged member through his trousers. His head spun and his heart raced. A groan of protest slipped from his lips when Andras broke from the kiss. Sweet Virgin, had he breached a boundary he shouldn't have crossed? His question was answered moments later when like before, Andras moved so fast, he knew not how they ended up on his cot in the corner of his abode.

A red aura rimmed the silver eyes as Andras removed his clothing and then looked at him. "Yours. Take them off, everything."

Lying side-by-side, Owen felt the heat from Andras's naked body as he fumbled with the buttons on his linen shirt. A strong, steady hand reached out to assist him in freeing the buttons before he rolled the trousers from his hips, his touch shooting through him like a surge of lightning. By the time all his clothing had been removed, he'd ceased to think.

"Now, continue on with what ye started," Andras said. "Ye wish to know my body?"

Owen licked his lips and nodded.

"Ye shall have your wish, and then I will know yours—every inch."

He ran his hand down the smooth, velvety length of Andras's member and stroked it, slow at first as if to memorize the breadth and width. Emboldened by the man's moan, he increased the tempo and felt it expand and harden.

It wasn't enough. He wanted—no, needed to taste him until the blood sang in his head, savor his essence, and commit it to memory. Sliding down the length of his sculpted body, he exchanged his hand for his mouth. He licked his tongue over the bulbous head and experienced his first taste of another man's essence.

Delirious, he lapped it up and then wrapped his mouth around the swollen shaft, this time eliciting a string of pained whimpers from Andras. His lips became brazen, his tongue demanding, and Owen reveled in the thick, solid warmth of his sex.

Owen felt a gentle tug on his hair. "Ye must stop or this will be over before it begins. I've waited too long for that to occur."

Breathing hard, Owen looked up and wondered what would happen next, every muscle in his body stretched taut. He'd only dreamed about loving Andras, had no real knowledge about what transpired between lovers.

Andras brushed his hand across his chest, found a nipple and rubbed the sensitive bud between his thumb and forefinger. A strangled moan left Owen's lips, the depth of his desire for the man astounding him. He lowered his head and suckled Owen until he writhed beneath his skillful mouth. With the taste of Andras's lips still fresh on his, Owen licked them and decided the man tasted wholesome and earthy, like pine needles from the Bunya tree.

Andras flipped him onto his stomach as if he maintained the weight of a house fly. Stuffing the lone pillow under his hips, Owen felt him nudge his legs apart with his knees. His body tensed, every nerve vibrating with aching need. With one hand, Andras caught his right hip, with the other he spread his butt cheeks and slipped a finger inside. Owen groaned and his body trembled under the sudden invasion of his most private part. Andras held him firm and continued to stroke him, sliding his finger in and out until Owen rocked beneath the wicked intrusion and pushed back against his hand.

Mindless with indescribable desire, a series of groans left his lips and the blood rushed to his head.

Lights danced behind his eyelids and a vibration of wild pleasure thrummed through his blood.

A protest registered in the back of his mind when Andras removed his finger, then a rush of exquisite heat engulfed him when the exquisite man entered him. An initial flood of pain and burning swept over Owen, replaced moments later by pleasure. His body convulsed and gasping breaths came from his lips as inch by delicious inch he took him.

Shudders claimed him as Andras plunged and withdrew. Owen wanted everything he had to offer, had wanted nothing more than to touch him, lick him from the moment he first saw him. He arched his back and rode the crest of immeasurable bliss, their bodies blending like the night sky and the stars.

Andras raked his teeth along the sides of his neck while plunging into him with precision-like thrusts. "Ye have bewitched me," he whispered against his hot skin.

The words turned Owen's world on its axis and pushed him over the edge. His hands clenched the bed clothing and a dizzying rush of light sped through his brain. A veritable flame licked over him, searing his body and dazzling his brain. Screaming for release, he left his own mind and shuddered beneath him, imploding from the inside out, shattering like a falling meteor crashing to earth. Consciousness hung in a precarious balance; he'd never experienced anything so potent.

In the back of his dazed mind, he heard a bestial groan erupt from Andras's throat. His lover's body jerked when he drove his cock deep inside him final time and then collapsed on top of him.

The aromas of sweat and sex mingled in the air. Andras pulled out and drew him into his arms. His heart racing out of control, Owen buried his face against the rock- hard chest and struggled to regulate his breathing.

When he came back to earth, he looked into Andras's eyes. "Duw help me, I had no idea it would be so pleasurable."

Andras brushed a finger over his lips. "Duw help us both. We've crossed a river we shouldn't have forged."

"Do not say that; not after what passed between us."

Andras's hoarse voice and heavy-lidded gaze drew him like a hapless moth. "What passed between us, Owen, tell me?"

He'd tell him anything he wanted to hear, and more to earn his touch again. "I'm at a loss to explain it. 'Twas blissful, otherworldly."

"Aye," Andras uttered. "And whatever world we were in, I'll hunger to return time and again with ye."

Long minutes later, Owen broke the silence. "What brought ye to my abode tonight?"

"Not good news, I fear."

"Something has happened to Carys or Ifan, the babe?"

"No, Carys is well, and a wet nurse has been found for Ifan."

"'Tis a relief. Carys runs the risk of losing her heart to the boy should she care for him much longer." When Andras didn't answer, he pressed him. "What troubles ye so?"

"Glynnis Hale has died."

Owen pushed up onto an elbow. "The vision was about her."

Andras drew a deep breath. "Apparently."

"More will die."

"Do the visions tell ye how?"

He shook his head. "Nay, so ye must tell me how she died."

"Slain by vampires."

Icy fingers of fear crept up his spine. "Ye are certain?"

"I saw the puncture wounds in her neck. I would recognize them anywhere."

He drew the words out; didn't want to hear the answer, but knew he must. "This Dagan ye spoke of has arrived in Pembrokeshire?"

"Aye, and there's more to impart."

Silence loomed between them until Owen could no longer stand the deafening void. "Whatever it is, tell me."

"The villagers suspect ye."

The statement knocked the breath from his lungs, although it shouldn't have. Of course they'd suspect a sin eater when dealing with the macabre. "I must tend to Glynnis; absolve her sins."

"'Tis too risky, and doubtful the young and innocent Glynnis requires the services of a sin eater. If anyone saw ye in Abergwaun now 'twould fuel their suspicions."

Accepting Andras's logic, he nodded. "Ye told me once ye had assistance. Who aids ye?"

Andras dismissed his question with a shake of his head.

"If ye don't tell me, I will convince ye to turn me, hound ye until ye can't stand the sight of me."

"Imparting the information of who aids me could put ye in danger. The less the demonic Underworld knows of their enemies, the better chance of survival."

Owen turned Andras's head by cupping his chin, arched his own head back and bared his throat in his face.

Andras moaned and yanked his head from his fingers. "Ye promised we would not speak of turning ye."

"Nay, ye demanded; I did not swear an oath. Choose. Tell me who aids ye or I will continue to bare my neck in your stubborn face at every turn."

With an anguished groan, Andras said, "An unlikely benefactor, an armament that possesses the mysticism of my ancestors."

An image of the sword Owen stumbled across in the stables loomed behind his eyelids. "The sword that once belonged to Owain ap Gruffydd Fychan, the Prince of Wales?"

"Ye know of him?"

"My father schooled me in Welsh history." His tone apologetic he said, "The night I slept in your barn I found the sword and held it in my hands. Forgive me."

"There is nothing to forgive. Bellamy has it in his safekeeping and convinced me to awaken its supreme powers."

"That's how ye were able to defeat Traherne?"

"Aye, without the steel, I am but a turned vampire, a humble physician. " Andras snorted. "Although Traherne knew of the blade's magick, he believed his was stronger."

Owen dropped his gaze, his words as hollow as his heart. "Dagan seeks not only revenge for his tad's death, but covets the sword?"

"He'll not rest until it falls into his hands." Andras searched his face. "The weapon also allows the insufferable ones to walk in daylight if they shoulder it."

Stunned by the admission, he drew a sharp breath. "More will die before this is over."

Andras closed his eyes, the gesture confirming Owen's worst fears. "I must leave; Carys waits with Glynnis and I promised to meet with the villagers in the morn."

"Will ye come to me again?"

"Aye, when panic and terror subsides." Conviction

marked his next words. "'Twould be easier to stop breathing than to hold myself from ye now."

Owen managed a tremulous smile before Andras rose from the cot and dressed. He turned to him one last time as if to hold the image of his face forever.

And then the vampire disappeared from his abode like fog rolling out to sea.

Chapter Seven

A breeze pushed through the open window. Dagan stood before the altar in the northwest tower of the castle, prepared to pay homage to his master in the Underworld. The ceremony would be brief, yet borne of heartfelt pleadings for the Dark Lord's sanction.

With the thought that Johan and Emmett should return soon, a curse fell from his pinched lips. The wrath of Satan would fall upon his underlings' heads if they hadn't succeeded in carrying out his simple orders.

He placed the silver dagger with its black hilt on the altar, willed the candles to life and bowed his head. "Ye are in my subconscious, great liege Lord, ever present, never ignored, and always there. To the omnipotent giver of life, nay immortality, I beseech thee to come to my aid, place in my possession the weapon that allows us to walk free among mortal fools.

Whatever flows through your body, flows through mine. I am in your likeness, he who feeds on the warm, red elixir of life. I am the dreaded vampire, a blessed composition of your energy, lust and desire. My day is the mortal's night, my sustenance their blood. When earth has witnessed its last day, I shall rise again and serve ye for all eternity.

I come to ye now knowing I am but a weak servant at your everlasting mercy. Deliver the sacred weapon unto me, Dark Lord, so I might serve ye, go forth and do your righteous bidding. This I ask in the name of my sire, Traherne, your faithful servant. May his damned soul rest forever by your side in the glory of Hell."

Footsteps echoed in the chamber outside the tower. Dagan lifted his chin and waited for his lieutenants to enter.

Emmett led; his cerulean eyes glazed over with the

aftermath of slaked lust—a good sign. His strong, square jaw and flawless features fell under a stream of light from the wavering candles, evoking a surge of nostalgia in Dagan. Of all his kin, Emmett bore the genetic likeness of his father.

Johan followed, his dark hair shining like polished wood in the dim light of the tower. Dagan focused on his eyes—the color of hazelnuts—and knew his father's nephew had not killed this night, but had been the one to follow Andras.

"Success," Emmett said, bowing before the altar.

"Pray tell."

"One less villager to contend with and her death has incited the reaction ye desired." "Panic and suspicion, the crème de la crème combination, but not enough to force Maddock's hand yet."

Dagan tapped an impatient foot against the marble floor. "Continue."

"After the girl was slain, I waited near the corpse until her father found her." A crimson flash marked the blue of his eyes as if Emmett called to mind his blood feast this very moment. "A touching scene. The man roused the entire village with his mournful wails and then led them to Maddock's abode at the top of the cliff."

"Ye followed, of course?"

"Aye, the girl's mother accused the sin eater of slaying her daughter. Maddock came to his defense as did a lass who goes by the name of Carys. The physician convinced them to return to their homes, and on the morrow the local justice of the peace would begin his investigation."

"Ye did well, Emmett." Dagan shifted his gaze to Johan. "Do ye also deliver good tidings?"

"My Lord will rejoice upon hearing it."

Dagan smiled. "Spare no details."

"I remained at my post outside Maddock Manor, heard his ward, Carys, beseech him to warn the sin eater, a lad by the name of Owen."

Dagan rolled his eyes, his vexation apparent. "Spit it out."

"Shortly thereafter, Andras left his dwelling and took flight. He paid a visit to a neighboring village." Johan snorted. "Stopped at an abode outside the village proper."

"I knew it! And does this whore have a name?"

Fidgeting with his fingers, the words tumbled forth. "He did not call upon a whore."

"Speak, man. Who then?"

"The sin eater."

Dagan gave him a sidelong look of disbelief. "He meant to warn him? Ye are mistaken. Andras would not waste his time with a sin eater no more than any mortal fool would." He skirted the altar and stood before them. "Perhaps he called upon the sin eater to administer to the girl?"

Johan shook his head. "It would not take the man two hours to convince him."

A long pause ensued before Dagan tossed back his head. "Oh, this is rich!"

"I thought ye'd be pleased."

"Do ye recall my words...every man has a weakness? Although I admit to being shocked by his choice of whores, we found Maddock's."

Johan nodded. "What do ye wish us to do now, my Lord?"

Dagan looked toward the window. Outside, the rim of the sun breached the horizon in vibrant shades of ochre and gold. "Rest, of course, and resume your duties at sunset."

"Kill another?"

"And another and another until the villagers are

convinced a madman lives within their midst, preys upon their innocent children."

"The sin eater," Emmett asked.

"Of course. Maddock will not be able to control their rage and he can't confess to his vampiric life lest they turn on him."

Johan scratched his head. "I fail to see how it furthers our cause if they kill the sin eater."

"The very reason I lead in my father's stead. Before the over-zealous villagers kill the sin eater, I'll barter his life for the sword, save him from a most gruesome death."

"Why do we not just take the lad now and exchange his life for the weapon?"

Dagan masked his annoyance with deceptive calmness. "Maddock is no fool. He'll fight to win him back...with the sword. No, he must surrender the weapon first if he hopes to see the lad alive again."

Emmett and Johan exchanged anxious looks as the first rays of the morning sun filtered across the floor. "Johan, ye have earned the honor of the next kill. Did ye get a glimpse of what Maddock's object of desire looks like?"

"Yes, my Lord. I watched him play the cwth from the stoop of his abode." Under his breath he added, "He plays the devil's fiddle to be sure; never heard the likes of it."

"Charming, however, I couldn't care less about his capabilities. Assume his identity and do try hard to leave a witness—alive, of course." Dagan turned to Emmett. "Find Alvaro before ye seek rest and tell him to relieve Kale tonight at the gatehouse. I grow weary of his whining."

"Has he seen evidence of lycans in the area?"

"None, as I suspected."

With a wave of his hand, Dagan dismissed them

and headed for his crypt with the sweet taste of victory on his tongue.

* * *

Fitful dreams invaded Andras's sleep, wound through his slumber without a moment's respite. The wind keened through the forest, its morose howl carrying a sinister portent of death. Onward he ran; his legs heavier than the Castle Blarney stone. Leaves swirled and twisted behind him as if caught up in an eddy of superhuman strength. His foot caught a hollow log, pitching him headfirst onto the narrow path. The smell of damp earth spiraled up his nose with a scent so spellbinding, it paralyzed him.

With great effort, he raised his head and terror struck his heart. Long, white teeth flashed behind a malevolent smile, transforming the magnificent features of the vampire's face. Ribbons of scarlet snaked through the cerulean eyes and Andras couldn't seem to tear his gaze away. The black cape descended and hovered over him like the wings of a mighty vulture.

Andras bolted upright in bed, his body drenched in sweat, his heart thundering in his chest. He reached for a glass of water on his night bureau, downed it in one swift gulp, and willed his wild heart to calm. Would he ever be free from the nightmare of Traherne's attack in the forest?

Knowing sleep would elude him now, he rose from bed, dressed and glanced at the mantle clock. Seven o'clock in the evening. Carys would arrive soon to inform him the Hales were in the study waiting to speak with him.

After returning to the manor at daybreak, he'd conducted his examination of Glynnis and his suspicions were confirmed. Not a drop of blood remained in her veins and the puncture wounds in her neck were too symmetric to have been left by a wild beast. Rarely did an animal attack a human, but on the occasions that he'd witnessed it, large gaping wounds marked the corpse where the flesh had been ripped from the body.

He slumped into the overstuffed chair by the hearth, rested his elbow on his knee and dropped his chin into his hand. Erotic images of Owen crept like spider legs through every cell of his body, surging through him like scalding embers. How difficult it had been to harness his immortal lust last night. It had taken every ounce of his will to squelch the powerful urge to sink his fangs into the tender flesh of his neck and sate his animalistic cravings. He knew what had stopped him, an overwhelming need to protect Owen from all things evil, including himself.

A subtle rap at the door, followed by Carys's angelic voice drew him from his musings. "Andras, the Hales have arrived for Glynnis."

"Tell them I'll be down."

The echo of her footsteps fading in the hallway reached him. He slid his arms into his waistcoat and buttoned it. Soon Glynnis's parents would remove their daughter's body from the manor, hold a wake at their homestead and wait three days before they buried her. Watchers would be employed to sit with the body while the parents prayed to the Almighty, hoping it was all a mistake; their lass wasn't gone forever, but rendered unconscious.

Nil chance of that.

At the end of the three-days—after the watchers had failed to rouse her through witchcraft and black magick—the wailers would arrive to lead the procession to her burial place. They'd beat on their chests, call out her name three times, and chant like specters until Glynnis was lowered into the ground. The Welsh seldom deviated from their customs and beliefs.

Nausea swirled in Andras's stomach. How could he tell them Glynnis had died at the hands of a vampire? Welsh lore abounded with changelings, the fae and other supernatural creatures, but for the village physician to admit that long tooths walked among them would incite a riot. Questions would arise. Did he have firsthand knowledge of the puncture marks left on her neck? Where was the proof the blood had been drained from her body? Legend and lore were one thing; attesting to the presence of vampires, another.

Above all, he had to protect Owen. Like Glynnis, an innocent caught up in a tangled web of deceit and subterfuge, the masquerade unfolding had nothing to do with him. Abhorred by the superstitious villagers as a thing unclean by reason of the life he'd chosen, they had jumped at the chance to lay blame at the sin eater's doorstep. Somehow, Andras had to shift that blame to the real culprits without pitching the neighboring villages into reckless hysteria.

How to accomplish the feat escaped his befuddled mind.

Andras gathered his scattered thoughts, left his bedchamber and bounded down the stairs to meet with Glynnis' parents in the study. The sound of a bugle-horn wound through the air and froze him in mid-stride. He'd heard the same eerie blare the previous night just before the villagers had arrived at Maddock Manor with Glynnis.

Mother of Jesus, it means one thing—another has died.

Carys and the Hales met him in the foyer, their faces etched in terror. Andras opened the massive doors and with his companions in close pursuit, left the manor. His heart fell to an unknown place below his knees. A crowd had gathered on the brow of the knoll, their desolate wails drifting skyward toward star-studded clouds.

The masses parted to make way for Tomas Evans carrying the limp body of Bronwen Carnes in his arms. A series of shrill shrieks from the girl's mother, the widow Carnes, rent the night air as she hobbled forward on Tomas's left side. The local justice of the peace, Geoffrey Tibbett, had taken up a position on Tomas's right side, his face somber.

Andras rushed toward the lad, not failing to notice the deep gash across his forehead. "What happened?"

"We were attacked near old Caffyn Manor last night." A sob escaped his trembling lips. "I've walked all day carrying Bronwen. Can ye do anything for her, sir?"

Andras looked down at the girl, sheer black anguish sweeping through him. Like Glynnis, the time had long since passed to save her. Her long auburn hair cascaded over Tomas' arms, leaving him a clear view of her neck. Two distinct, perpendicular marks branded a spot near her jugular vein.

"I'm so sorry." Andras looked at her mother, his voice choked with emotion.

"Nay, she's all I have left." She lifted her eyes toward heaven. "Do not take her from me; I beg of ye, Duw."

The crowd had joined them, their faces glowering with rage, their raised fists punching the empty air.

Tibbett stepped forward. "Tomas caught a glimpse of the killer before he knocked him unconscious."

Andras held his breath and searched Tomas's face. "Aye, 'twas Owen Rhys, the sin eater."

From beside him, Carys fell to her knees and Mistress Hale shouted, "Did I not tell ye it was him responsible for my Glynnis's death? And now he struck again."

"Kill him! Kill him!" the crowd roared in unison.

"Hang the unholy monster by the neck until dead!"

another shouted.

Andras grabbed Tibbett by the elbow. "Geoffrey, I beseech ye to stop this hysteria. 'Tis not the doing of Owen Rhys."

The justice put his hand in the air and appealed for calm. "Cease now, we must listen to what everyone has to say. Panic will get us nowhere. Ye," he said pointing to two stout males from the village. "Take this poor girl from Tomas and cover her so she's decent."

Andras's blade smith, Bellamy, stepped up with a blanket from the stables. "Allow me, son." He waved the villagers off and took her from the boy's arms. "Turn her over now; that's a fine lad." After a serious nod to Andras, Bellamy walked toward the manor with the dead girl.

Tomas ran his hands through an unruly lock of hair at his forehead and grimaced when his fingers made contact with the wound. "He hit me with a sturdy limb. I heard Bronwen scream and lights flashed in my noggin." His eyes narrowed. "I lost my senses for a long time, but not before I looked into the devil's green eyes."

"Ye said he hit ye on the head first, lad." Tibbett placed a hand on his shoulder. "Were ye able to get a good look at him, or do ye think ye might have been a wee fuzzy?"

"I saw him as clear as the fingers on my hands. 'Twas Owen Rhys, the sin eater. I'd know that face anywhere. Though he bears a likeness to Michael, the Almighty's archangel...." he crossed himself. "he's spawned of the devil."

Boos and jeers echoed among the crowd and bile rose in Andras's throat. Beside him on the ground, Carys shook her head and turned a tear-stained face to the angry mob. "'Tis not possible, I tell ye. I've lost two of my dearest friends, yet I know in my heart the sin eater is not capable of such vile acts."

The village wood-turner sneered. "Ye dare to defend the most unholy?"

The widow Carnes ceased her mournful outburst long enough to interject. "He keeps goats, does he not?"

"Aye," said Mistress Hale. "'Tis rumored the creatures cavort with the Tylwyth Teg and Diawl."

Through thin lips, Carys said, "Ye know better than to say such things, Mistress Hale. Goats are held in high esteem here and even if they do communicate with the fae, the fair people are harmless for the most part."

"I'll wager we'll find his bloody clothes should we journey to his abode."

Andras didn't bother to look toward the voice. He did all he could to keep the contents in his stomach from spewing from his throat.

Geoffrey turned and faced the angry mob. "Nobody is to journey anywhere, except mayhap Doctor Maddock." He looked over his shoulder and addressed him. "Ye know the lad best from your dealings with him upon the deathbed. Do ye think ye can convince him to come in with ye?"

Andras nodded. "I'll do my best."

"What then?" Edward Hale's voice rose above the chatter. "My lass is dead, and now the widow's. Before another is killed, he must be locked away."

"Do not tell me of my job, Edward. We'll hold a Quarter Sessions as soon as I'm able to round up another justice of the peace. The sin eater will have a fair trial like everyone else—two justices, a chairman and a jury."

Andras breathed an internal sigh of relief. It would take Geoffrey a week to gather the appropriate members to hold a Quarter Sessions. Before then, he'd think of some way to prove Owen's innocence. If he had to hunt Dagan down, kill him and haul his soulless carcass into the village, then so be it.

"Now go home, folk. The good doctor will examine Bronwen and make a full report to me. I swear to ye the sin eater will be behind bars by morning."

Andras looked at a dazed Tomas. "Come to the manor and allow me tend your wound."

The crowd dispersed, but not before Geoffrey had a final word for Andras. "Ye have until morning to bring him in. Don't disappoint me."

Andras helped Carys to her feet and led her and Tomas into the house, doing his best to control the anger pressing down on him.

Chapter Eight

The air thick with the smell of treachery and death, Andras soared above rain- infused clouds. Moments later, he stood on the sin eater's stoop reliving last night—the intoxicating musk of Owen's sweat-soaked skin, the hard, lean curves molding to the contours of his own body; mostly, the memory of his hungry mouth devouring Owen's.

He closed his eyes and wondered if the rich, chestnut hair would be tied back tonight with a strip of leather or falling loose about his shoulders—wild and free like the man himself. He had to find the strength to cast aside this uncontrollable passion he harbored for Owen. Like the ill-fated love of Heloise and Abelard, theirs was doomed.

The melodic notes of a fiddle drifted through the open window, its haunting melody wrenching his gut. As if Owen sensed his presence, the music stopped and then the door opened. Their eyes met and locked across the short expanse before Owen graced him with a smile designed by Duw. Andras felt his bestial heart stop for a beat or two.

Wild and free. Owen's hair hung loose, tumbled down his back in waves of carnelian silk. His eyes glistened in reflected candlelight and Andras couldn't decide if the luminous orbs were a shade of emerald or sapphire at the moment.

A horrific image flashed behind Andras's eyelids—Owen hanging from the gallows, the grotesque angle of his neck a mockery of its prior grace. A black hood covered the thick, silken locks and a mask of the same color concealed his sculpted features. Andras fought the strangled cry of frustration lingering on the tip of his tongue.

The words fell from Owen's lips on a whisper. "I

didn't think to see ye again after...."

"Ye weren't listening, then."

Andras saw the shift of perception cross the green-spoked eyes. "Ye are not here of your own free will, are ye?"

He shook his head and summoned his courage. Owen stepped aside, and with a flourish of his arm bade him enter. "The night is chilly. Be seated at the table and I'll prepare tea."

Andras slid into the chair, his mind congested with raging emotions. Never had he felt so helpless. He studied Owen whilst he steeped the tea leaves and then poured the steaming water through a muslin sieve.

After setting a mug before him, Owen settled into a chair across the table with the grace of a fawn and wrapped his hands around his own cup of tea. "'Tis best not to dangle your toe, but submerge the whole of your foot once committed."

"Your father's words?"

Owen nodded.

"Very well." Andras rushed the words. "Bronwen Carnes is dead."

A whoosh of air left Owen's lungs. "My tad did not say to submerge the whole of your body at once."

"I'm a straightforward man."

A slight smile bracketed his mouth. "'Tis good to know."

"Dagan or one from his clan found her and Tomas near the old Caffyn Manor."

"The abandoned stone farmhouse?" Owen gave another subtle smile. "'Tis poor reasoning to find humor at a time like this, but I didn't think the reticent Tomas bold enough to lift a lass's skirts."

"Aye, nor I, but we misjudged him."

"And what of Tomas?"

"Knocked on the head, but unharmed."

Owen looked to the cross hanging on the wall beside his mother's likeness. "I pray Bronwen has joined Glynnis and they dance with the faeries under Duw's crab orchard." A tense silence enveloped the room before Owen spoke again. "Tomas has named me a murderer. Is that not what ye came to tell me?"

There were times Andras believed Owen had entered the world possessed of supernatural insight. He saw things, felt things others did not. What a travesty the villagers considered him an uneducated, lowly outcast, an unholy pariah by virtue of his vocation. In reality, the complexity of his spirit stood heads above them all. Owen Rhys was a composite of old souls and new, a perfect blend of the arcane and the avant-garde, and Andras had fallen in love with every multifaceted fiber of the man's being.

"Tomas said he saw your face before entering the dream world. When he awoke, he carried Bronwen into the village hoping it wasn't too late to save her."

Owen rose from the chair and paced. "This madness must stop! Surrender the sword to Dagan and he'll leave Pembrokeshire."

"Are ye daft? He'll not leave; they'll slake their bloodlust night and day. There will be no respite from their malice if they're allowed to walk in daylight."

He turned to him with his hands out at his sides. "There is no respite from their malice now. More will die before this ends."

"I must go to the authorities with the truth. 'Tis the only way."

"'Tis ye who is daft now." Owen gave him a derisive snort. "Surrender the one thing in your life that matters most to ye? Ye took an oath to minister to the sick. If ye confess the truth to the authorities ye lose everything."

Andras slammed his fist on the table. "Don't

presume to tell me what I must do!"

His tone laced with sarcasm Owen countered. "It would solve nothing. How far will ye run this time?"

"Far enough so they'll never find me."

The tense lines on Owen's face relaxed, although he continued his harried strides.

"Such a place does not exist, Andras. Traherne followed ye here and his son now takes up the gauntlet. Go ahead; tell them vampires walk among us, bare your soul about the attack in the woods, and to what good? Your work here will be for naught, and Dagan will hunt ye down again and again."

"Ye are mistaken about—"

"I'm not mistaken!"

"—one thing."

Owen stopped in mid-stride, his eyes the deepest forest green as they met his. When he swallowed hard, his Adam's apple slid up and down.

Andras's chest constricted. "My practice is not what matters most to me."

"What, then?" he whispered.

"Ye, Owen—more than the sun, the stars, the very air I breathe."

The sin eater walked toward him; his eyes filled with moisture. "Andras, do not tell them, I beg of ye."

"I must; it's the only way."

Closer now, a hair's breadth away, Owen looked down on him. "I'll not allow ye to ruin all that ye have accomplished here in Pembrokeshire. If ye make this false statement—"

"False! 'Tis not false and ye of all people know it."

He slid into Andras's lap with his knees hugging both hips. "If ye make this false statement, I'll swear an oath I killed Glynnis and Bronwen. Ye know the folk will believe the most unholy over the beloved physician. I'll tell them I hit Tomas on the head while he lay with

Bronwen in the tall grass outside Caffyn Manor, detail the wound marks along her neck. If I wasn't the culprit, how would I know of such things?"

"They'll hang ye from the gallows quicker than ye can cross yourself if ye confess to these crimes."

"Aye, and ye will have no time to come up with a way to defeat Dagan once and for all."

"Remove yourself from my person. Ye trapped me."

"Nay."

"Nay? Ye wish me to remove ye by force?"

Adopting a bold persona, his eyes glistening like jack pines after a summer storm, he lowered his voice. "By force, aye."

Shadows danced over the angular planes of his face, and the very air they breathed hummed with profound vibration. "No good can come of this thing between us. Ye must know that as I know it."

"Ye want me, Andras, have wanted me for a long time." Owen's sweet, warm breath fanned his lips. "I've seen the way ye watch me when ye think I'm looking elsewhere."

The room spun in shades of silver and gold and Andras's blood turned to liquid fire. Owen's hot, probing tongue sought the depths of his mouth and his hand slid down to the hard shaft between his thighs. Through his trousers, he kneaded the pulsating member and ran his thumb over the sensitive head, drawing an involuntary moan from Andras.

"Ye want me," Owen said into his open mouth. Running his tongue over his bottom lip, he drew him into that endless chasm Andras feared, yet craved. "Deny it and I'll remove myself from your person."

Waves of hunger shot through him. *God, yes, I want ye, more than anything I've ever wanted in my life.* He grabbed a length of Owen's hair at the back of his head and, forcing it back, exposed his neck. "Should I show ye how much I want ye, possess ye, mind, body and soul?"

"Do it, Andras." He arched his neck back further, goading him. "I don't fear ye or your power. Make me like ye and I'll help ye defeat this monster holding our future in his hands."

Tormented by the beast within, fighting a powerful urge to slake his bloodlust and claim Owen for all eternity, Andras's mind swam through a sea of conflict. Owen's graceful, slender neck lay exposed to his fangs and how he hungered to bury them in that tender flesh.

"I beg of ye, do it."

He released his hair so abruptly, Owen's head bobbled. Glazed over with unspent desire, confusion masked Owen's eyes. "Take your clothing off," Andras said. "Everything. Ye have awakened the beast, but I will not succumb to my bloodlust. I will appease my hunger by possessing your body in a way ye will never forget."

Owen tugged the linen shirt over his head, and only then did their mutual gaze break for a timeless moment. Andras's cock wept as he lifted him from his lap and flipped him around until his waist hugged the table. A clear view of his naked back rose before him.

"Lean against it with your arms bearing your weight, palms down."

Owen complied in silence and Andras rose to stand behind him, not touching him, but rather savoring the hard, lean lines of his body—the muscled biceps, broad shoulders and narrow waist. Duw, had he died and gone to heaven? One of the worst days of his life had just turned into one of the most astonishing. Andras kicked his feet out until Owen's legs were spread wide and then he slid a hand over his bottom.

A shudder rippled through Owen and his body tensed. Andras reached around with his free hand and found his manhood, aware of the rise and fall of Owen's ragged breath as he slid his hand up and down the full length. The hot flesh throbbed and his essence moistened the tip. Andras spread the liquid around with his fingers and kneaded the damp slit.

Whimpers fell from Owen's lips—the sound pitching Andras over the edge. His taut bottom pushed back against his thighs. Andras's hand slid to cleft between his cheeks, his finger roaming between the mounds until he found Owen's entrance. He slid a finger inside.

Owen cried out and bucked forward. "Oh Duw."

"Want me to cease?" Andras asked calling on Duw himself, hoping Owen hadn't changed his mind.

"More," he gasped.

Unable to pull his gaze from the decadent view, Andras pulled his finger out, slipped two in and probed amid a series of staccato moans from Owen. He repressed his own shiver and concentrated on the window over his cot. If he didn't pace himself, this would be over in a heartbeat . . . the last thing in the world he wanted.

Owen's insides pulsated against his fingers and his hips thrust back to meet his assault. Andras could no longer bear his own arousal. He removed his hand from Owen's hard shaft, unbuttoned his trousers and freed his manhood. His usual, unshakable control threatened to defeat him. Lust simmered in his veins, semen ran from his tip and glistened down the length of his erection. He watched the taut muscles of Owen's forearms quiver as he removed his fingers, positioned the tip of his shaft at his entrance and exalted in the potent trembling of raw hunger.

"Is this how ye wanted me to possess ye?"

"No. Yes," he panted.

Andras entered him, burying the head. An animalistic groan spewed from Owen's throat, and only when the tight muscles of his insides relaxed to adjust to his width, did Andras begin to move.

Owen thrashed beneath him and a guttural groan from his belly escaped when Andras pushed in and buried his cock to the hilt. His arms collapsed and his face fell to the table. Andras grabbed his hips with both hands, retreated again and drove in hard and fast. Owen cried out, and a haze of pleasure unlike any Andras had ever known spread through every limb, like an all-consuming fire that stripped his soul bare.

Owen undulated beneath him, his sleek, chestnut hair glistening under ribbons of muted amber and gold from the candlelight. His body spasmed and Andras knew the lad's release grew imminent.

"Don't stop, not now, harder, faster."

His own balls tightened and he felt hot liquid rush to the top of his cock. He couldn't think, aware of the beautiful man beneath him and his throbbing member buried inside him. Hovering at the pinnacle of insanity, Andras reveled in the sound of another bestial groan from Owen. His hands rough on the feverish skin of his hips, he yanked him back hard against his body and slammed into him with one final thrust.

Owen cried out and Andras's own release came in an unending echo of bliss, the power and intensity of his ejaculation blinding him. He collapsed against Owen's damp body, aware of a groan from somewhere deep inside his gut. Long minutes later, after his breathing had returned to normal, Andras whispered into Owen's ear. "That's the only way I'll ever possess ye. I beg ye, don't ask me again to turn ye."

"Then don't ask me to remain silent while ye intend to offer yourself like a sacrificial lamb," Owen said between ragged breaths.

"Ye are a stubborn jackass." Andras lifted himself from the splendid body and buttoned his trousers.

"Aye," he replied rolling over onto his back to face him. "I fear them not. Did I not tell ye once they can't kill me because I'm already dead?"

"Don't talk such foolishness. A mortal who can bring such joy to a long tooth can't be dead."

Owen plucked his shirt from the table and slid it over his head. "How long do we have before I must return with ye?"

"How did ye know?"

He smiled. "Like the long tooth, I read minds."

Andras smiled in return. "Till morning."

"Come." Owen took him by the hand and led him to the cot. "'Tis time to tell me about your home and family. I want to know about your life before ye arrived in Pembrokeshire."

Chapter Nine

The village jail didn't differ much from Owen's abode. An adjunct of Tibbett's residence, four dank walls, and a lone pine writing table, a wobbly chair and several beeswax candles had kept him company for six days now. A tiny window encased with metal bars—compliments of the village brazier—provided the only natural light.

Taking great care not to touch any part of his person, Tibbett's wife delivered his meals, one to break his fast in the morning, one at midday and a light repast in the evening. Tonight, she'd entered his gloomy chamber with a tray of pan-seared marlin and a crust of fennel rye. Her obsidian eyes piercing him with a wary gaze, she'd set the fare down on the table, crossed herself and walked backward from the cell.

With a sigh of boredom, Owen shuffled to the window and looked at the orchard of yews guarding the boundary of Tibbett's property on his right. Looking left, the village of Abergwaun came into view, not so very different in appearance than his village, Wdig. Situated on the river Gwayn, near its influx into St. George's Channel, some of the largest vessels arriving into Abergwaun's port carried trade from Bristol, Liverpool and London. He didn't have much understanding about the internal workings of either village, but his sire had lived by the creed that knowledge put the world in a man's hand.

What are ye thinking now, Tad? Have ye forsaken your son for this love he harbors for another man? Can ye hold it in your heart to forgive me?

He narrowed his eyes and focused on the village stocks. Here offenders were shackled for days, much to the scorn and laughter of onlookers. Reserved for those who'd committed petty crimes, at least he'd be spared that humiliation. Aye, the gallows awaited him should he be found guilty of killing Glynnis and Bronwen.

Eleanor Tibbett's clipped voice drew him from the window. "Ye have a visitor."

His buoyant mood at the thought it might be Andras dissolved when Carys appeared behind the stout woman. She waited until Mistress Tibbett made her exit before passing a book through the metal bars.

Stumbling through false bravado, her eyes moist with tears, she said, "'Tis a novel by Maria Edgeworth entitled *Castle Rackrent*."

He thanked her with a nod and set the book down on the table.

"Do not fret about your goats," she added, her lower lip trembling. "I see to them every morn."

"Set them free, Carys. I've no further use of them."

He wanted to retract the words when a single tear slid down her cheek. "'Tis black luck to speak thus. Andras says ye will not see the gallows. He's given his word."

"Someone must pay for Glynnis's and Bronwen's deaths; why not the sin eater?"

The girl looked at him with a gasp. "Do not say it; do not think it."

He pushed a hand through the bars and brushed away her tear. "Carys, ye must accept whatever happens to me. I wish for ye to be happy."

"A justice has arrived from Abergavenny and the jury has been selected." Her eyes darted about and her voice wavered. "Andras puts little stock in their fairness. He claims they are biased against prisoners, their sentences severe."

"The outcome 'tis already written." He shrugged with detached inevitably.

"I'm frightened, Owen." She looked over her shoulder to make sure old lady Tibbett hadn't taken it in her head to eavesdrop. "Andras has taken up the sword again, as he did when we left Castle Sycharth and first came to Abergwaun. He spends his nights with Bellamy in the stables."

The sound of his name fell over Owen like a caress. "'Tis beautiful, his ancestral home?"

"There are few words to describe the beauty of the land." Her eyes clouded with visions past and her expression turned pensive. "At one time the castle crowned the summit of a hill and boasted a stone bridge with five arches."

Owen tried to picture it in his mind.

"The castle was torched four centuries past by King Henry V, but Andras's grandfather constructed a fine manor home near where the motte and bailey once stood." She faltered in the sudden silence engulfing them. "One day this will be behind us and ye will see Castle Sycharth through your own eyes."

If only her words were true. He didn't want to think about it, couldn't allow himself to venture there. Not when the whole world would soon tumble down around him.

She dug into the pocket of her dress, her eyes wide, and then passed him a pendant of some type through the bars. "Oh, I almost forgot. I've another gift for ye."

He turned it over in his hand and studied it. At the end of the leather string hung a matching pouch emblazoned with a silver cross. "What's inside?"

"Needles and bits of bark from the yew that stands on the west side of the churchyards." She lowered her voice. "Vampires fear the yew."

He felt his eyes brim with tenderness. "Thank ye, Carys. I'll treasure it always."

Mistress Tibbett's heavy footsteps echoed in the corridor before a tsk-tsk fell from her lips. "A body needs rest and 'tis long past my time to retire."

Carys offered a tremulous smile. "I'll visit again soon."

He called out to her before she reached the end of the corridor. "Place salt under your pillow, will also keep them away."

She nodded, and then she was gone, leaving him alone again with the misery of the night.

* * *

Owen bolted upright in his cot and stared into the dark recesses of his chamber. His senses filled with an eerie awareness of another's presence, and for a moment he wondered if he remained in the throes of a nightmare.

The candle on the table flamed and outlined a shadowy countenance in the corner, confirming his suspicions he wasn't alone. His sleep-drugged brain cleared and his throat tightened. A light sleeper, he hadn't heard the familiar clank of the metal bars opening and closing, which meant whoever had entered his cell, had come in through the narrow window.

Steeped in shadows, the figure stepped forward. "No," the otherworldly voice said with cynical inflection. "Your lover hasn't arrived in the dark of night. Pity, that."

His heart knocking in his chest, Owen resolved to keep his tone calm. "Which of Dagan's lackeys do I have the pleasure of meeting?"

For a long moment silence fell across the small space and the candle sparked, illuminating the most perfect face Owen had ever seen in his short life. Dark, of tawny complexion, and dressed in a light gray vest and matching waistcoat, a cravat of the same color in darker hues adorned his throat. A brooch of the finest silver embellished the tie and complemented the sterling links of his sleeves.

Faultless and defined, the features of his face were

framed by a waterfall of thick, dark hair that fell in waves past his collarbones. An aura of scarlet suffused the vibrant aquamarine eyes of mystery and power, dazzling Owen for a timeless moment even while his mind screamed *danger*.

"I wouldn't waste the time or effort dispatching a member of my clan. I had to see for myself the man Andras would give his life for."

The insolence of his tone fanned to life the dormant anger in Owen. He rose from the cot and faced him when the man, one slow step at a time, advanced. With the stealth of a predator he circled him once and then stopped inches before his face. "He'll die, ye know. Are ye prepared to live with his passing for the rest of your life?"

He countered icily, "Ye seem to have forgotten a minor detail. Andras possesses the sword."

His eyes blazed fire for a brief moment before fading out. "I'm most impressed, I must say." He raked him over head to toe before reaching out with a finger to touch his face. "I'll follow ye and make a heaven out of Hell, and I'll die by your hand which I love so well."

"Shakespeare," Owen said. "'Tis I who am impressed now." He flinched back and struggled to clear his head. The undead's strong powers reached inside his brain, threatening to overpower him.

"From whom did ye inherit the emerald eyes?" the vampire asked.

Owen met his question with silence.

"Your mother, no doubt, since I had the pleasure of seeing your sire once. Allow me to recall the encounter for ye. Bleeding out in the forest after my father sucked the life force from your beloved Andras, your father stumbled across the cur. He saved him in exchange for protection. *Your* protection. I watched and listened while the scene played out."

"Why did my tad save Andras?"

"Like ye, the old man possessed the sight, sensed his mortal life would end soon." A sinister laugh left his erotic lips. "Ye must know by now ye possess the sight? Oh, and so much more my young beauty. Well, getting back to your sire, he knew well the pathetic life of a sin eater. Perhaps he had a vision one day Andras would deliver ye from sharing the same fate—a misguided prophecy, I might add."

"Ye lie! My tad warned me to stay clear of Andras. 'Beware of the long tooth,' he said."

Laughter transformed the magnificent features again. "Gullible lad; he warned ye of me."

Forced to dispel thoughts of his father lest he crumble, Owen changed the subject. "What do ye hope to gain from owning the weapon?"

"Although it's difficult for me to read your every thought, it's not impossible. Do not feign ignorance with me. Andras told ye of the claymore's mystical powers and its ability to grant us immunity from sunlight." He tilted his head and leaned in, his warm breath fanning Owen's cheek. "With the sword, the insufferable ones will unite to form a nation and I, Dagan, son of Traherne, will lead them."

Owen took a step back and shook his head, his befuddled senses reeling. *Duw help me.* He closed his eyes, could no longer look into that arrogant face. "What do ye want of me?"

"The question becomes, what do ye want? I presume ye'd be stricken bereft should your beloved prince die. Ye can save him, ye know."

"How?"

"Convince him to give me the sword."

"Nay, he will not part with it."

"To save ye, he'd surrender his life. The Prince of Wales's sword doesn't hold such value to him."

"What if ye are mistaken?"

The crimson eyes glimmered. "I'm never mistaken." He took a step forward and grabbed Owen by the throat, the power of his grip cutting off his airway. "Let me prove it to ye. At this very moment ye are thinking of ways to thwart me. I'd advise ye to banish such notions from your mind. There's only one way Maddock will live to see the sun rise each morning." He paused and studied him for a lengthy time. "And that is to deliver the sword into my hands."

Owen gagged and chortled on the bile rising up from his stomach.

"And to ensure ye do as I say, allow my power to persuade ye."

Against his will, his mind yielded to the force of energy snaking through it. The vampire's thoughts became his, and his, the vampire's. The familiar mental anguish he'd lived with so long vanished like smoke. His spirit left his body and a mindless void enveloped him. He saw Dagan's beauty, felt a charismatic draw from which he couldn't break free.

The room spun overhead and his legs gave way beneath him. The long tooth's features loomed before him and then faded like an elusive wind. "Call out my name in your mind after ye've convinced Maddock to relinquish the sword. I'll hear ye and come."

Owen collapsed into the chair and gulped air like a fish out of water. Sensing he was alone again, he plucked Carys's adornment from the table. He tied it around his neck, concealing the pouch beneath his shirt. Curse his stupidity; he should have donned it the moment Carys passed it through the bars.

He scanned the cramped quarters in the dim light. The vampire had vanished, leaving an incandescent void in his stead.

* * *

His every thought on the sin eater, his libidinous cravings at their highest peak, Dagan rounded a corner in the tower and almost collided with Alvaro.

Taken aback, his underling's eyes widened. "Forgive me, my Lord, Estevan sent me in search of ye."

"He should have been searching for ye these past three days." Dagan eyed him. "I pray ye can account for your absence and your undertakings."

"Hunting in the woods, sire, nothing more."

"Ye are aware I issued strict orders not to feast upon the villagers unless I sanction it?"

Alvaro gave a gasp of denial. "I swear I've hunted the beasts of the forests. I haven't ventured into either village."

He pinned him with a stern glare. "And do not, lest all my best laid plans are unraveled."

"Plans, my Lord?"

"Yes, plans, ye dolt. I swear your rapacious hunger will never be sated. I don't care if one day it becomes the death of ye, but if your voracious craving for blood interferes in my life, I'll be displeased." Dagan straightened his clothing and walked into the inner chamber of the north tower with Alvaro dogging his heels.

"I apologize for my absence. If it pleases ye, enlighten me about your plans, my Lord."

A vignette of images rose in Dagan's mind—all of the beautiful man he'd just visited in jail. If he didn't take charge of his sudden obsession, he wouldn't have to worry about Alvaro unraveling the plan already set into motion. The devil take him, he'd never met a man who moved him so.

He wasn't concerned about the bestial instincts the boy had aroused, par for the course. No, Maddock's lover had stirred emotions in him that had long been dormant, sentiment he'd buried centuries ago.

Heat coursed through his veins and rushed toward his groin at the thought of possessing the one called Owen, claiming him for all eternity. Not since he'd lost Lyon three hundred years ago had he felt such passion. Centuries had passed and still the jagged, black pain had never abated whenever he thought of Lyon, his friend, his mentor, his lover. He'd never longed to fill the empty void, the deep cavern that existed after his lover's death, not until he gazed upon the face of the sin eater.

"My Lord?"

"Yes, it does please me to enlighten ye, so heed me well. At my direction, Johan and Emmett appeased their bloodlust on two hapless girls from the village. As expected, the chary town folk looked to the local sin eater as the culprit." He rubbed his hands together and smiled. "I just returned from visiting one Owen Rhys in a dreary structure while he awaits trial."

Alvaro licked his lips. "Tell me; was his blood rich, sweet, tainted with a coppery—"

"Unlike ye, Alvaro, I'm able to control my hunger if duty necessitates. In this instance, I need the lad alive." Dagan shuddered when another image rose of the breath-stopping face. To think of Owen as gone forever from the mortal world—no, from either world, mortal or immortal—impaled his icy heart.

"But why do ye need him alive?"

"All in due time, all in due time. For now, ye have been told all ye need to know."

Alvaro bowed his head. "Yes, my Lord."

"Gather the others and ask them to come to me at once. It's time we honor our liege Lord, thank him for the wondrous gift of immortal life."

Backing away, Alvaro asked, "What of Kale? His whining intercepted me for over an hour upon entering the gatehouse."

Dagan considered the odds of Andras finding them at Castle Carew while steeped in the dilemma surrounding his lover. "Yes, tell him I expect him at the ceremony. He should be grateful for the brief respite." Dagan stopped him before he reached the exit. "Tell me, while hunting in the woods, did ye happen to come across evidence of lycans in the shire?"

"None, great leader. Rest assured, I kept an eye out for their presence."

With a wave of his hand, he dismissed him. "Be gone and do what I asked of ye."

When Alvaro left the chamber, Dagan returned to his licentious thoughts of Owen, knowing they could never be more than that—whimsical daydreams he'd cherish forever.

Or could they?

The smoldering green eyes appeared amid the flawless features. Dagan pictured Owen kneeling before him, his tongue tantalizing his cock, eradicating his latent impotence. If anyone could convince the flaccid member to spring to life after all these years, the stunning man with the faultless body and extraordinary beauty could.

He imagined his bronze hand with its long, nimble fingers stroking his hard flesh. Owen would grace him with a smile, his eyes filled with unspent lust. More agile than any human, Dagan would twist his body around; arrange him as he pictured him now, in the massive four-poster on his hands and knees.

First, he'd caress every inch of that silken flesh until he writhed beneath his skillful ministrations, became as malleable as a piece of clay. Owen would thrust his bottom back against Dagan's hand, a silent plea to consummate this burning lust between them. His cock weeping and throbbing with need, Dagan would guide it to Owen's entrance, and with a powerful thrust, bury himself in deep.

The beautiful lad would arch his spine and fill the room with his base groans of pleasure. He'd close around him like a vise and beg for more...and more. And Dagan would accommodate him.

What a shame he might never know the man's desire. He'd love to explore the depths of his fantasies with a man who came along once in centuries.

Dispelling thoughts about what might have been, Dagan conjured a circle of fire around the altar in preparation for the pending ceremony.

Above the hiss of flames, his voice rang out, "In due time, all in due time."

Chapter Ten

"Hear ye, hear ye, the Quarter Sessions is now in order."

Andras scanned the packed courtroom, his gaze lingering on the angry expressions of those in attendance. They reminded him of jackals about to rip apart a dead carcass.

Seated to his left, Carys's face looked ashen against her patterned gown of pink roses and the deep plum, half-circle cloak enveloping her shoulders. She wrung her hands before folding them in her lap and offered him a tentative smile. Bellamy flanked his right in blatant, albeit unusual, support of the young sin eater he'd come to admire.

The noisy chatter in the room evaporated when Geoffrey Tibbett entered through a side door with Owen. Dressed in a pair of ash-colored trousers and matching linen shirt, his hands were shackled at the wrists. Geoffrey escorted the alleged murderer to an oak table in front of the raised dais where the justices and a jury of his peers were seated, and then he joined his comrades.

Geoffrey remained standing and addressed the silent crowd. "In accordance with an act of Parliament, the Wales and Berwick Act of 1746, all laws applying to England will likewise apply to Wales."

Geoffrey looked to Owen. "Owen Rhys, ye have been charged with the murders of Glynnis Hale, daughter of Edward Hale, the cordwainer of Abergwaun, and Bronwen Carnes, daughter of the widow Carnes of the same village."

Andras glanced toward the source of the angst-ridden hysterics after the girls' names were declared. Standing side by side, the widow Carnes and Glynnis's mother embraced, their gut-wrenching sobs stirring the crowd.

"Order," Geoffrey proclaimed, slamming down his gavel. "The Sessions will call forth witnesses before hearing the sin eater's plea. I remind ye we must have total silence during the hearing. Now then, the Court calls Tomas Evans."

The young man rose from a section of pews near the front and walked toward a table parallel to the one Owen occupied. Andras didn't know Tomas well, but from his dealings with the man, he'd never known him to fabricate the truth. Nor was he the type to bend his elbow in one of the taverns while spinning wild yarns.

Something was amiss, and yet Andras couldn't pinpoint the source. He'd spoken to Tomas several times and the man insisted he saw Owen Rhys's face before being knocked unconscious. He'd also examined Tomas's head after the incident and little doubt remained, he'd been knocked senseless, apparently during the time Bronwen had fought for her life.

Tomas eased into the chair at the table and looked up at the panel of Justices and jury, his face somber.

Geoffrey rose again and addressed him. "Now start at the beginning, lad, tell the Sessions what ye were doing at the old Caffyn Manor that eve."

Several loud guffaws rose in the room and a deep blush crept up Tomas's neck and stained his cheeks. "Passing time 'tis all we were doing. Bronwen had a yearning to gather cowslips and bluebells and knew of a patch growing along the boundary of the old manor house." He cleared his throat. "We thought no harm would come from taking a handful or two, so...."

"Yes, yes." Geoffrey grimaced. "Let's move on to what happened next."

Tomas squirmed in the chair. "Bronwen laid out a blanket in the tall rye grass and we meant only to pass the time in conversation."

"And?" Geoffrey pressed.

"'Tis a black wind that will chase ye down should ye speak ill of the dead."

"We're not asking ye to speak of Miss Carnes in an uncivil manner; we wish to get at the truth. A young man's life is at stake here, Tomas."

"Aye." He snuck a hooded glance at Owen. "Bronwen, that is Miss Carnes, took it in her head to steal a kiss."

Shocked gasps rose in the courtroom.

"A kiss 'twas all, nothing more." He hung his head, his voice dropping to a whisper. "She leaned over and before I knew what happened, someone knocked her clean off my chest.

One swipe of a hand and she went a sailing through the air."

A wail erupted among the crowd. Andras glanced to his right and saw the Widow Carnes weeping into a linen hankie.

Tomas continued. "The branch of a poplar appeared before my eyes before making contact with my noggin. White lights exploded in my brain and the sky spun overhead."

"Ye passed out, then?" Geoffrey asked.

"Nearly. Worried about Bronwen, I fought it; Duw knows I wanted to come to her aid."

"Where do ye think Miss Carnes was at that point?"

"Twenty-five feet from the blanket, northeast."

Geoffrey's brow furrowed. "Exactly twenty-five feet, not twenty feet or thirty feet?"

"No sir. I went back to Caffyn Manor two days later and walked off every step. The grass was bent where Bronwen laid the blanket down, and I knew she landed near a boulder."

"'Tis a fine job ye are doing, Tomas. What

happened next?"

"I saw him then, Owen Rhys, clear as daylight. Just before he knelt down by Bronwen, he turned and looked square at me. There's no mistaking those green eyes—'tis the mark of witchcraft and devilry."

A round of boos and hisses rose in the room.

A justice from the bench slammed his gavel down. "Silence!"

"As ye sit here today," Geoffrey continued, "there's no doubt in your mind ye saw the sin eater looming over Mistress Carnes that night?"

"Not a shred of doubt."

Andras glanced to Owen again. With his head bowed, he couldn't see his face, but he hadn't moved a muscle, hadn't shown the slightest reaction to Tomas's testimony.

"Very well, Mister Evans, resume your seat."

Tomas passed by the Widow Carnes and stopped to pat her shoulder.

"The Sessions calls Carys Vaughn."

Beside him, Carys rose from the bench and walked toward the table. Before settling into the chair she glanced toward Owen.

"Be seated, Miss Vaughn. I want to take ye back to a day the sin eater slept inside Maddock Manor. I believe 'twas the time of Mistress Davies's departure."

Carys nodded.

"Edward Hale claims Owen Rhys spied on ye, Misses Carnes, Hale and Daw from Andras's bedchamber whilst ye made corn dollies near the fountain."

"Wasn't spying; he was looking out the window."

"Ye admit to seeing him look down?"

Another nod before she looked over her shoulder at Tomas. "I admit to having green eyes too—a sign of devilry and witchcraft."

Shocked gasps drifted toward the ceiling.

"Tell me," Geoffrey said. "What was the sin eater doing in the physician's private bedchamber?"

"Resting after a fall. Doctor Maddock forbade him to make the journey home to Wdig."

Geoffrey paced before the table, stopping in front of it to ask his next question. "Don't ye find it peculiar the sin eater wouldn't retire to the stables?"

Carys stared him down. "No more peculiar than ye retiring the stables. Mayhap ye prefer the smell of horse dung to clean linen."

The room erupted in laughter while Geoffrey coughed, chortled and turned as purple as a plum. "Ye are defending a sin eater, Miss Vaughn!"

"I'm defending the truth!" She leaned forward, her eyes sparking fire. "Owen Rhys is no more capable of these crimes than a fly on the wall. I'll not condemn him, nor will I allow ye to coat my tongue with false words, Justice Tibbett."

"Blasphemy!" an angry voice shouted.

"The sin eater has bedeviled the lass!" another cried.

Carys placed her palms on the table and pushed herself up. "'Tis not true! By all that is holy, I swear 'tis not true!"

Andras was about to jump up and protest when Owen came to his feet. All heads turned in his direction.

"I plead guilty," he said low-voiced.

Chaos broke out in the packed room. Carys lowered her head and beside Andras, Bellamy emitted a curse.

Slamming his gavel down thrice, the head justice waited until the anger subsided and addressed Owen. "What did ye say, Rhys?"

"There's no need to call forth witnesses. I plead guilty to the crimes of killing Glynnis Hale and

Bronwen Carnes."

Andras came to his feet, unable to hold back the tumultuous emotions threatening to choke him. "'Tis a lie! The sin eater is not guilty of these crimes!"

The room exploded in jeers—raucous, taunting hisses aimed at Owen. "He confessed, and rightly so," a voice called out.

"Construct the gallows!" another rang out. "Hang the bastard!"

"Silence!" Geoffrey roared.

Andras's stomach knotted and his throat closed up. He left the pew, walked to Owen, and stood so close their shoulders touched. "What in hell do ye think ye are doing? Retract your plea this instant."

Refusing to meet his eyes, Owen shook his head.

"Ye didn't kill those girls; ye and I both know it."

Owen lifted his head and looked into his eyes. "Aye, I did."

"Ye lie!" he said hissing the words between clenched teeth. When Owen failed to react, he softened his tone. "I know why ye are confessing, and I won't allow it to happen. Do ye hear me? I'll tell them the truth...here, now."

He'd never heard such defeat in any man's voice. "They won't believe ye, Andras. Look at their faces. This is what they want, so I'll accommodate them."

Andras faced Geoffrey. "He confesses to crimes he didn't commit."

"Unless ye have evidence that another carried out the crimes, the Sessions must take his plea as fact."

"I'll provide ye with factual evidence proving Owen Rhys did not—"

Void of emotion, the green eyes held his gaze. "I've confessed to the crimes, Justice Tibbett. According to English law, ye must accept my plea and mete out my sentence."

"No!" Andras yelled. "Do not sentence him until—"

"Andras, the court has no choice. The sin eater has confessed to the crimes he's been charged with. The justices must pass sentence." Geoffrey slammed his gavel a final time. "Having pled guilty to the murders of one Glynnis Hale and one Bronwen Carnes, this Quarter Sessions sentences ye to be hung by the neck until dead. Your punishment will be carried out at sunset tomorrow in the village proper."

Over his shoulder, Andras heard Carys cry out. "No, please, Owen is innocent of these crimes!"

The crowd came to their feet; their shouts and jeers overriding Geoffrey's frantic pounding of the gavel. "Adjourned! This court is adjourned!"

Before Andras had time to speak again, Tibbett appeared beside them. "If ye hope to keep him alive until tomorrow, hold the crowd back while I get him out of here, Andras."

"Geoffrey, this is a mockery of the justice system. Ye can't allow this to happen without affording him a proper trial, admission of guilt notwithstanding."

"I had no choice, Andras. If I'd refused to pass sentence after his confession, this angry mob would have hung him now and we couldn't have stopped them." He placed a hand on his arm. "If ye have evidence another committed the crimes, bring it to me before sunset tomorrow. If not, may his soul rest in peace."

Andras looked into Owen's eyes a final time before Tibbett led him away, the sinking anguish in his chest immeasurable. In numb disbelief, he turned and walked toward Carys, the last traces of docility vanishing from his heart.

By the time he and Carys had joined Bellamy, the man met his hardened features with a knowing look. "Prepare the Prince's sword," Andras said. "The time for battle has come."

* * *

That night, after comforting Carys, and confident she'd retired to her room for the night, Andras sat in his bedchamber and stewed. He alternated between wearing out a path on the Persian rug and looking out the window at the full moon, his mind teeming with unanswered questions. Owen's words from their last night together refused to leave his head, 'Don't ask me to remain silent while ye intend to offer yourself like the sacrificial lamb.'

He knew why Owen had confessed—to spare him the devastation of having to admit to the entire village he was a bona fide member of the undead. 'I'll not allow ye to ruin all ye have accomplished here in Pembrokeshire,' he'd said. And oh, God, he'd said more, so much more. 'Ye want me, Andras. I've seen the way ye watch me when ye think I'm looking elsewhere.'

He couldn't allow him to die. To even think such a thing crumbled him. So little time remained to save him, but save him he would. He'd never cared what the villagers thought; he had only intended to keep his oath to help the sick and dying. His practice meant nothing to him without Owen. Hell, life held no meaning without Owen. He knew that now more than ever.

He left his bedchamber and walked outside with the niggling fear something had been amiss when he'd looked into Owen's lifeless eyes that morning. The strong connection between them had been fractured - he sensed it, felt it with every fiber of his being. Nothing in the mortal world could break the chains binding them. Andras reeled back as if struck by lightning. Only a supernatural force of the highest measure could tear down the impregnable link between them.

Dagan.

The moon blanketed the land in an arresting

display of radiant light. He looked at the stars and swore he heard the sweet music of Duw's harps strumming out a mournful tune. An omen? A foreboding? He couldn't think of that now; he had to speak to Owen, force him to admit Dagan had paid him a visit. And then he'd find the black cur and his bloodthirsty vampires if he had to turn the countryside upside down. He called on the heavens for help. "Give me one sign. Light the path and show me where the cowardly dogs hide."

A short time later, Andras stripped, pushed his clothing through the bars and slipped through the window of Owen's cell in the form of a crow and then transformed into the man again. Shallow, steady breathing from the single cot came to his heightened hearing.

As if on command, Owen glanced up and drew in a shocked gasp.

"Do not call out. The lanterns burn in Tibbett's abode yet."

Owen nodded and glanced at the sword hanging from a scabbard at his waist, next to the fiddle Andras carried in his hand. His fiddle.

Reining in his volatile emotions, Andras walked toward him. "What did ye hope to accomplish this morning when ye confessed?"

"I told the truth," he squeaked out.

"Ha! Ye forget I can read your thoughts most of the time." He tried to read them now and failed. Another sign Dagan had paid him a visit, had manipulated his mind.

"The truth, I want the truth, and ye are going to give it to me."

"Ye won't win, not even with your precious sword. He's more powerful than ye ever imagined."

"He came here, didn't he?" Met with silence,

Andras pressed onward. "He manipulated your mind, holds ye enthralled with his unearthly beauty and deceptive charms. Ye must fight it, not allow it to happen."

His voice raised an octave. "'Tis not about his beauty or his deception."

"What then? Tell me so I might help ye."

"The only way ye can help is to deliver the sword onto him. He'll spare your life and mine." His tone desperate now, he continued. "Give him what he seeks and everything will be as it was before."

"Will it? Can it bring Glynnis and Bronwen back from their cold graves? Will Carys remain safe from vampires till the end of her days? What about the innocent children of the village?"

"Yes, yes! Dagan has sworn to leave if I convince ye to bring him the Prince's sword."

"It will not end there. Ye don't understand their kind."

"Your kind, ye mean!" he spat the words.

Grim resignation marked his words. "Yes, my kind. 'Tis why I know it will not end until Dagan and his clan are wiped from the face of the earth."

"Andras, please, I beg of ye; don't seek to battle him. Ye will not win."

"Did he tell where they stay in Pembrokeshire?"

He shook his head. "Nay, he warned me not to thwart him, said he'd kill ye if I even think it."

"I'll deliver him into the Shadowland of Hell for threatening ye."

Like glacial ice, the green eyes hardened. "I don't want ye to defend me or...." He hesitated and his eyes darted about the cell. "Care about me. Whatever passed between us is over. I no longer want ye."

Andras's eyes clung to his, analyzing his words while trying to read his mind. Nil. Nothing. Dagan had done a fine job of controlling his thoughts. The seconds ticked by. Owen dropped his chin and Andras studied him—the fringe of his long lashes against his sculpted cheeks, the alluring mouth, and the long chestnut hair glimmering beneath streaks of silver moonlight.

"This habit ye have acquired of lying is beginning to annoy me."

"I speak the truth."

Andras reached down, grabbed him by his shirt and yanked him to his feet. "Let us put it to the test." Crushing Owen to him, he took his mouth with savage intensity. Owen parted his lips allowing him full access and a pained moan came from the back of his throat. Long moments later, Andras broke from the kiss, pushed him back against the wall and pinned him there. "Tell me again ye no longer want me."

* * *

Caught off balance, Owen stepped back and became trapped between a barrier and a mass of muscle and strength. Reeling from the savage kiss, the sane part of his body recognized Andras's manhood pushing into his pelvis.

His last shred of control disintegrated. He tore at Andras's shirt to remove it from his torso, and then slid his hands up his chest. A moan escaped Andras's lips and the man's heart beat out of control beneath his palm. It wasn't enough to just touch that smooth skin. Owen wanted to taste it again, every inch.

His hands worked with increasing feverishness to free the buttons on Andras's trousers. "Please," he said, frustrated.

Andras unbuttoned his own trousers, slid them down his hips and next removed Owen's. His legs giving way, Owen dropped to his knees and Andras's hard shaft came into view, large, hard and begging for his mouth. He licked the head amid the man's strangled moans.

Winding his fingers in a lock of his hair, Andras applied pressure. "Suck it," he said. "Take me into your mouth."

Owen devoured the pulsating cock, taking it in so deep it hit the back of his throat. Heaven, pure heaven. Andras's scent spiraled up his nostrils—the decadent aroma of arousal and pure male. His own hard flesh throbbed in perfect sync with his impassioned sucking. Andras's hips ground against his mouth. "Harder," he rasped.

More than eager to please him, Owen set upon him, drawing out the retreat and surrender in measured strokes. Mesmerized by the man and everything about him, he withdrew his mouth, licked his lips and ran his tongue down one side and then up the other.

Tiny beads of liquid leaked from Andras's tip, the heady scent enticing Owen, luring him to wrap his mouth around his cock again. Owen's heart hammered in his chest. He'd never felt such a rush, not even the first time he'd tasted Andras. Tremors wracked his body; the anticipation of what would come next too overwhelming to think about.

Andras's hard shaft pulsated in his mouth. An innate sense told him the magnificent being struggled to hold his release in check. He bucked and groaned, inciting Owen into a faster tempo.

Lost in the dark depths of hunger and need, Andras's voice came to him through a tunnel. "Get down on your hands and knees. Now. Hurry."

Owen's hands shook as he wrenched his shirt over his head, counting off the seconds in his head until Andras would be inside him. On his hands and knees, his muscles cramped along his spine and he struggled to keep his body from caving in. Thank Duw, Andras took over and slipped an arm under his waist before he could form his next thought. A groan left Owen's lips when Andras slid a finger inside his hole and probed. He tried to lift his head, but Andras held him in place. "Easy, Owen, I won't hurt ye."

"Hurt me? The only way ye will hurt me is if ye cease."

He removed his finger and pushed two inside Owen, eliciting an animal-like groan from him. While pummeling him with his skilled fingers, Andras reached for his sacs with his other hand and caressed them. Jolts of exquisite sensations surged through Owen and his release crested. On the edge of a fathomless precipice, Owen focused and drew several deep breaths. He didn't want this to end. Ever.

Andras removed his fingers and nudged his entrance with his cock, the sensation sending him into a new wave of tremors. Grasping him tighter, a hoarse cry left his throat when Andras buried himself hard and deep. Owen moaned, the pleasure and pain intense, mingling until he couldn't distinguish one from the other. His body jerked under the exquisite man's tortuous assault—a measured plunder of deep, hard thrusts. All traces of pain ebbed, replaced by a mind-numbing ecstasy that left him dazed.

Sweat streamed from his forehead and the muscles in his legs and arms screamed out in protest. He pushed back to meet Andras's hard thrusts, taking him in to the hilt.

Hot semen spurted from his shaft, fierce, intense, and in perfect time with Andras emptying his seed into him. Weak, his breaths coming in hard, short bursts, Owen collapsed against the floor and felt Andras's full weight on his back.

Andras ran his warm tongue over the outside of Owen's ear. "Don't ever tell me again ye no longer want me."

"If I can make ye respond in such a manner, I'd be a fool not to." Spent and weak, Owen didn't protest when Andras picked him up in his strong arms and carried him to the cot. "Don't leave me."

Andras reached down and slid his hand over the hair at the side of his head. "I don't want to leave ye, but I must. Six hours remain before daylight and I've an entire shire to search."

"What if ye don't find them?"

"I won't let ye die, if that's what ye are asking. Ye have my word."

His eyes droopy, his mind dazed, Owen responded with a groggy, "Hmm."

"Sleep, beautiful lad. Dagan will not come to ye tonight."

"How can ye be sure?" He yawned.

"The vampire's awareness is heightened when someone hunts him. He'll not make himself visible now."

"Be careful, Andras, promise me."

Owen opened his eyes seconds later and wondered why Andras hadn't answered him, but the man had vanished like the mist at sunrise.

Chapter Eleven

Dagan's howl of rage shook the stone walls of the northwest tower. "I should rip your throat out with an awl, sever your brainless skull from your body with a dull knife!"

Alvaro stood before him, his muslin shirt a patchwork of crimson stains and gore. "Forgive me, my lord, I had no idea she resided in Abergwaun."

"Ye fool! I said ye were not to feast on any human without my sanction!"

In an attempt to defuse Dagan's wrath, Estevan stepped forward, his shoulders wilting under his leader's tirade. "Perhaps her body will not be found for a day or two."

"Do ye think me addle-brained? If a young woman goes missing now, the entire village will turn out to search for her." The heels of Dagan's boots clattered against the marble floor, the velocity of his pace a blur. "So close, so close until your insatiable thirst for blood extinguished our chance for victory."

Alvaro dropped to his knees, his voice quaking. "When I saw her bathing by the stream, I should have run, I know that now, but...."

"Don't dare to offer feeble excuses. Do ye think ye are the only undead who struggles to control the beast, rails against overpowering cravings? We must all, on occasion, sacrifice for the good of the clan, answer to a higher calling."

"Yes, sire."

Dagan walked toward him, grabbed a fistful of silver hair and yanked his head back.

"I'd kill ye with my bare hands if I didn't require your services right now." For emphasis, he leaned down, his face inches from Alvaro's. "And serve me, ye will."

A long breath escaped Alvaro's lips. "Anything, anything ye ask of me, my Lord."

Dagan straightened his body and looked to his other minions—Estevan, Emmett, Johan and Kale. "Prepare to leave for Abergwaun within the hour." Emmett met his gaze. "The sin eater has summoned ye?"

"If Rhys had somehow convinced Andras to relinquish the sword, do ye think the death of one wretched villager would concern me? No, the sin eater has not called me forth. I can assume he's willing to sacrifice his own life in favor of the greater good." His venomous glare shriveled Alvaro. "Which is more than I can say for ye."

Alvaro hung his head again.

"When the woman's body is found, they'll realize Owen Rhys did not kill the others."

"What is the significance of such an act?" Kale asked.

"They'll set him free." Dagan tossed his head back and released a mordant laugh. "Worse, the revelation will send them down another path to find the real killer."

"Sire, forgive my lack of insight, but why hasn't Andras told them vampires stalk the night in Pembrokeshire?"

"Because he is one, ye dolt." Dagan looked toward the domed ceiling, its gilded panels glistening beneath the soft candlelight in the chamber. "I won't allow him to win."

"Do we go to Abergwaun to force him to give up the sword?" Emmett asked.

Dagan shot him a toxic glare. "I would have done so already if the possibility existed.

No, he'll not relinquish the Prince's claymore unless I'm in possession of something he loves more."

Johan raised a dark eyebrow. "What is that, my lord?"

Dagan's anger evaporated as he walked toward the altar, steepled his pale fingers and bowed his head. Images surfaced and an ache in his groin spread upward into his belly. Mayhap his darkest fantasies about the stunning lad would come to fruition after all.

Another vision surfaced. The mere thought of fighting Maddock for the sword sent a shiver of fright down his spine. Under normal circumstances, he'd crush Maddock's skull with one blow, rip out his throat and finish the job his father—"

"My lord?"

"Yes, yes, I heard your question. Here's my answer—he loves the sin eater more than the sword."

* * *

Dagan had been summoned.

By his liege lord, and the very thought of it stampeded his chest with breathless palpations.

He descended into the dark realm where sub-zero temperatures and armor-plated reptilians rose from the toxic sludge to snap men's bones in two. Here, gargantuan gargoyles and one-eyed-two-headed monsters wander the shadowy corridors on a quest to destroy life in any form.

Only once had he been beckoned, the day his clan retrieved his sire's broken body from the forest. Never had he seen such a vast empire of impious sin and enmity, had no desire to ever see it again. He couldn't ignore the summons, risk his Lord's blood-searing fury. The insidious lizard might take it in his head to consign him to the realm for all eternity. Curse Alvaro and his voracious appetite for blood. I should have severed his head from his worthless corpse and delivered it to the Lord of the Underworld à la carte. Perhaps it's not too late.

He loathed the stone walls slick with moisture and kept to the main passageways, aware of stirrings on his left flank. A squalid odor burned his nostrils, a mingling of algae, dank water and decomposing sea creatures. The chamber door ahead opened without his assistance. He walked forward, beset by another wave of noxious scents—seared flesh, stale mold, and fresh blood. The latter inflamed his senses, fanned his maddening frenzy of cravings. No oversight on his lord's part. He meant to torment him, bring him to his knees for any faux pas he'd committed.

From a corner of the chamber, piercing red eyes, fringed with ice-encrusted savagery, locked with his. "Dagan, my most humble servant, to what do I owe this honor?"

On bended knee, and taken aback by his question, he faltered. "Ye-ye summoned me, my lord."

The dragon emerged from the shadows, all slime-encrusted scales and fiery crimson eyes. He tossed the remainder of his meal—the leg of prehistoric vertebrate—aside and retracted his elongated tongue. "Ah yes, so I did. Distracted by more important matters," he looked at the remnants of his meal, "it slipped my mind for a moment."

Dagan willed his wobbly knees to still. "Tell me how I might serve ye."

A snort left his wide nostrils. "Ye disappoint me, Dagan. I thought ye were prepared to step into your father's role, but perhaps I was mistaken."

A rush of air left his lungs. "No, my Liege Lord. I assure ye things are progressing according to plan."

He arched his neck back, the stream of fire from his nose scorching the ceiling. "One of your minions has disobeyed your orders, and yet ye allowed him to live."

"I need him, my Lord, in order to obtain the sword."

A humorless laugh left the amphibious lips. "Minions and servants are dispensable," he said, the yellow-rimmed irises hardening. "Just as ye are dispensable."

A shiver straightened Dagan's spine. "I'll kill him and deliver his head to ye on a platter should ye command it."

"I'm not concerned about his death, or whether he still draws breath for that matter, but more so in the way ye lead."

"I would ask for another chance, My Lord. It will not happen again; ye have my word."

The incandescent sheen from the dragon's massive body quavered under the torchlight. "Little time remains to secure the Prince's sword. A battle looms on the horizon. Without the sword, my legions will not win." He paused and lowered his head, his serpent- like tongue flickering in and out. "Have ye any idea how it will upset me if my army doesn't reign victorious when all is said and done?"

Dagan nodded.

"While my powers extend beyond the boundaries of time, cross realms and dimensions, there's one *vexata quaestio* that hasn't been answered."

"What vexing question is that Sire?"

"The historic battle was fought under a blazing sun. If we intend to alter the course of history, it's imperative my legions are granted immunity from its harsh rays. And, what is the one object in all of creation that will grant them such sanction?"

"The Prince of Wales's sword. Your legions will prevail; they must, sire."

"Then hear me well, ye sniveling underling!" His thunderous voice reverberated throughout the cavern. "If the Prince's sword is not delivered to me within a fortnight, I'll hunt ye down myself."

"Yes, sire." He came to his feet. "The disobedient one, Alvaro, my lord?"

"As ye claim, ye need the cur for now. The moment ye have relieved Glyndŵr's heir of his sword, kill Alvaro."

"Ye have my oath."

"Leave me; I grow weary of coddling worthless insufferables. I should have sent the lycans in your stead, or perhaps my regiment of zombies. Had I followed my instinct, no doubt the sword would be in my possession at this very minute and ye wouldn't be standing before me wearing your white-livered spleen on your sleeve."

Dagan backed out of the chamber one slow step at a time, and turned when his heels clanked against the stone door. He turned, pushed the air through his trembling lips, and scurried along the passageways, thankful he still drew breath.

Chapter Twelve

Owen's view from the narrow window of his cell framed the rugged crags in the distance, a pleasing combination of cloud-hung peaks against a vivid blue sky. Goose flesh rippled over his skin when the mournful cries of the bagpipes drifted down the main road of the village, followed by the hair-raising cries of banshees—wailers leading Glynnis's and Bronwen's funeral procession.

Debilitating pain washed over him. He pictured the girls now the day he looked down at them from Andras's bedchamber. Glynnis, with her long golden locks and eyes the color of robin's eggs, a stark contrast to Bronwen's russet hair and brown eyes reminiscent of chocolate.

Pine caskets in the back of wagons drawn by piebald horses, the grieving parents and a horde of weeping, angry villagers passed by his cell. He covered his ears against the bone-chilling shrieks and wished the world would swallow him up.

Carys brought up the rear of the march, and veered off when she spied him, scurrying to the window. Her face wan, her eyes puffy, she brought her pale hands to the bars. "How do ye fare today, Owen?"

"'Tis a horrific thing to witness, the wailers."

"Aye, if I live to be a hundred it will never set right with me."

"Ye shouldn't be here, Carys. They'll shun ye for speaking to the sin eater."

"Let them." Anger flashed in her eyes. "I want to leave Abergwaun and never return. 'Tis a town filled with hate."

"Nay, 'tis not hate ye name, but superstition and fear."

She chewed on her lower lip. "I have my own fear

to deal with this morn. Andras didn't return home last eve and hasn't shown his face this morn. He wouldn't miss the burial unless something terrible happened."

Owen's gut clenched. "He can take care of himself, lass. Don't worry your pretty head about something ye can do nothing about." How he wished he could take his own advice.

"Mistress Hopkins claims to have seen Gwrach y Rhibyn this morn while washing clothes in the stream." Carys drew in a sharp breath.

"Old woman Hopkins is wrong in the head. She always claims to see the Hag of the Mist."

"Just the same, she swears she heard her shriek of misfortune or," she swallowed, "death."

"And whose name did the Hag call out?"

Tears pooled in her eyes and she looked away. "She wouldn't say."

Owen crooked his finger in hers, drawing her gaze again. "The hag called out my name, did she not?"

"Oh, I'm so frightened. Andras is gone and the vampires...." She crossed herself. "The vampires will come and kill us all if something has happened to him." An edge of defiance mingled with her fear and rode the edge of her voice. "Don't deny the truth, Owen Rhys. Andras told me one set upon ye in the woods, and he had to slay the insufferable one to save ye."

He looked down; his voice quiet. "Andras shouldn't be filling the head of innocents with such babble."

"Innocents! I'll have ye know my dear parents were attacked when I was but ten, killed by werewolves, the elders say. After that, I could no longer claim to be an innocent. Look at me, Owen," she said and then met his eyes. "When the undead set upon Andras, he told me. Bellamy knows too, so stop treating me like a child."

"Ye must listen to me now; there is little time left. Andras will return. When ye have paid your respects to Glynnis and Bronwen, go home and sit with Bellamy in the stables until he comes home."

"Very well." She wiped her tears away with the back of her hand. "Ye didn't forget to hang the pendant around your neck, did ye, Owen?"

He pulled it out with his thumb as an image of Dagan surfaced. "Nay, has protected me well." Her eyes lingered on his face for a lengthy time. "What is it ye wish to say?"

"If Andras doesn't return," a sob broke her words. "Bellamy and I will somehow set ye free."

"Nay! 'Tis too dangerous. Ye mustn't even think it."

"I can't bear it if they hang ye."

"Carys, sweet, sweet Carys, I'm twice blessed to call ye friend."

"Twice blessed?"

He nodded.

"How so?"

"Once for your beauty, another for your loyalty."

She smiled through tears again and his heart wrenched. He couldn't tell her Andras had left to hunt down Dagan and his clan. She'd launch into an apoplectic crying jag if she knew the truth. And he couldn't let her know he was also worried about Andras not returning. The whole world seemed to be on fire now and there wasn't a thing he could do about it. Except smile at Carys in return. "Go now, and may Duw go with ye."

"And ye," she said kissing his hand through the bars.

He watched her walk away, slumped into the chair and sent a silent prayer toward heaven.

Then he picked up his fiddle and lost himself in

the woeful tunes he loved.

* * *

Andras slipped through the back door of the stables at twilight. "What in hell are ye about, Bellamy?"

His friend spun around and breathed a sigh of relief. "Took ten years off my life sneaking through the back door, and where in Diawl's name have ye been?"

"Nay, I asked first. Why are ye dressed like a brigand about to go on a raid?"

Bellamy spread his arms out and sketched a bow. "Because I am about to go on a raid to save the sin eater."

Andras couldn't help his smile. "One man against an angry mob?"

"Aye, I must do what I must do." He raked him over with a discerning eye. "And look who calls the kettle black? 'Tis the devil's colors ye wear head to toe. The villagers will run like specters have taken hold of their souls when ye show your face."

Andras stifled the protracted smile. "They'll run when they discover a vampire in their midst."

"Do ye know what ye are about to do?" Bellamy asked blowing air through his lips.

"What other choice do I have? Were ye planning to march up to the gallows, cut him free, and then what? Your intentions elude me."

"I haven't gone that far in my thinking but I can't abide in hanging him." Bellamy closed one eye. "There's no taking it back once ye disclose what ye are."

"I can think of no other way to save him. I've searched every cavern, copse and bog in the shire for Dagan."

"Without success?"

Andras shook his head. "The miserable undead possess the ability to conjure a refuge in any location, underground if they choose." Placing a hand on his shoulder, he added, "I thank ye for your devotion and concern."

"If ye spend much longer thanking me, the lad will be looking for a remedy to cure his broken neck."

"Aye, on to lower town to thwart their hanging of an innocent."

"I'll be right behind ye," Bellamy said with a firm nod. "I prefer to travel by my own means."

Andras headed for the back door, turned and faced him. "What of Carys? The lanterns are doused in the manor."

Slapping his forehead, Bellamy emitted a disgruntled groan. "I told the lass to wait for your return. I should have insisted she stay with me."

He closed his eyes for a moment. "Stubborn girl. She'd never allow him to die alone."

Andras left the stables and looked skyward. Dusk rode the wings of daylight, and soon night would fall upon the shire. A heavy portent shadowed his heart. This day could never be taken back, whatever was about to unfurl, he couldn't stop. He no longer cared about the oath he'd taken to ease the suffering of the sick. All that had been taken from him five years ago. The time to make his stand had come. Win or lose. Owen wouldn't die by the hangman's noose, and he'd soon appear to the folk in his true form, show them what he really was.

A vampire, the most feared demon of the Underworld.

* * *

The miserable day dragged on for Owen with the speed of a tortoise crossing a gravel road. He'd played every tune in his repertoire twice before Mistress Tibbett brought his midday meal, a mash made of potatoes, carrots, turnips, peas, parsnips and leeks. And a fresh glass of milk. The fare had all the makings of a dying man's last request.

The sound of hammers driving nails into pine boards drifted through his window. The villagers were constructing the gallows—his gallows. In several hours he'd come face to face with either Duw or Diawl.

Perhaps the folk were right. By virtue of his unholy occupation, he wouldn't make it to heaven, if there was a heaven. He knew Uffern existed; his short days on earth could be likened to Hell. His father often spoke of Annwn, the otherworld of delights and eternal youth, free of earthly disease where food is abundant. "The land of souls that departed this world," he'd called it.

Minutes before sundown and still no word from Andras or Carys, Owen accepted his fate. On his knees in front of the dingy cot in his cell, the thud of heavy footsteps echoed down the corridor.

Tibbett unlocked the bars and entered with the parson, the man who lived near Andras in upper town. "'Tis time, Owen," Geoffrey said.

Ruddy-faced with a grizzled beard, his long robes covering everything but his shoes, the cleric knelt beside him. "Place your hand on the Holy Book and confess your transgressions."

Owen hesitated. For the life of him he couldn't think of a single sin he'd committed other than this abiding love he held for another man. The silence lengthened while Andras's face surfaced and all the dark shadows in his heart vanished. Nay, he would not confess that sin. How could something borne on the wings of rapture be evil? "I've nothing to confess." He rose, turned to Geoffrey and held out his wrists. "I'm prepared."

With great effort, and using the small table to hoist himself up, the parson rose and shook his head. "Ye had little chance of entering Duw's kingdom before. Now ye have none."

Geoffrey shackled his wrists and led him from the cell. Outside, a crowd had assembled, every man, woman and child from Wdig, Abergwaun and perhaps a neighboring village or two tossed in for good measure.

Owen looked at the sun dropping on the horizon with profound appreciation for its beauty. In its wake, a full, glorious moon rose in the sky to stand guard over the heavens. He'd miss the celestial objects and their magnificent transformations.

Vying for a better view of his execution, the crowd shifted en masse as Owen, the parson and Geoffrey walked between two parallel lines leading to the scaffold. He scanned the faces of the villagers hoping to catch a glimpse of Andras. Despair washed over him. Had his soul already fled from earth? Was he lying somewhere with Dagan's dagger embedded in his heart?

Carys's face loomed before him. "Owen, look over here!"

At the sound of her voice, he found a sense of calm and smiled at the girl with eyes the color of pine needles.

Her expression determined, she elbowed her way through the crowd, glancing over her shoulder now and then to keep him in sight. "Keep your eyes on me. I'm here for ye, Owen."

Lovely Carys, the lass with a smile that could make the angels weep. She'd come for him, the sin eater, to bring him comfort in his last minutes on earth. A moment of panic caught him unaware. Checking himself, he marched onward. He wouldn't show them cowardice, wouldn't tremble or beg for forgiveness. If he could find and hold Carys's face among the masses, he'd die like a man.

The steps to the gallows rose before him. He counted them off in his head, and upon reaching the top of the platform, looked for Carys.

"Here, I'm here, Owen," she said patting her chest.

He drew a deep breath and watched Geoffrey pulled the black hood from the pocket of his trousers.

And Owen took a last look at Carys.

Chapter Thirteen

Owen made his peace with Duw and allowed his last thoughts of Andras to filter into his brain. He'd relived every minute in his final hours, every conversation, Andras's touch and so much more. He closed his eyes and focused on the images—the man's tongue licking his skin, his soft groans of impatience before he possessed him.

He'd die with Andras's features etched on his brain.

A hushed silence came to the crowd when a hideous lament of grief rent the air. Owen opened his eyes and like the rest of the onlookers, craned his neck toward the eerie sound. He recognized the man by his towering height and noticeable limp—Sayer Daw, the village stone mason. Repeating the horror of the last several days, Daw walked forward cradling a sagging body in his arms. None could mistake the pale blonde hair his daughter Tarren was known for.

Owen had thought the premonition haunting him throughout the day related to his death, not that of another young woman.

"She has the mark of the long tooth on her neck!" Sayer shouted above the docile gathering. "Come see for yourself."

The women and children drew back, but several men rushed toward Sayer, leaned over her limp corpse, and examined her pale slender throat.

"'Tis the mark of the insufferable to be sure," a voice called out.

A unified gasp rose. Women clutched their children to their bosoms and scanned the outskirts of the village.

"Two puncture wounds from a beast," another said.

All eyes fell upon Daw as he walked toward the gallows and faced his friends and neighbors. "I'll wager we'd find the same wounds on Glynnis and Bronwen should we exhume their bodies." He turned and looked up at Owen. "The sin eater didn't kill Tarren. Locked in a jail cell when she was murdered, it would have been impossible."

Another round of shocked gasps followed.

"Where's Andras Maddock?" Geoffrey called out, searching the dumbfounded faces. "He can tell us whether the same wounds appeared on Glynnis and Bronwen."

Owen's breath hitched when Andras stepped into the clearing. Black as the night around him, leather breeches framed his narrow hips. An ebony shirt with billowing sleeves and a jerkin of the same color hugged his muscular torso. Pewter shields adorned his knees and forearms, and at his waist, the hilt of the Prince's sword glistened beneath moonbeams. His long midnight hair, tied back with a thin black rope, contrasted with the penetrating silver orbs.

Seized by the power of his magnetism, Owen couldn't take his eyes off the man.

The crowd swiveled at the sound of Andras's voice. "Aye, Bronwen and Glynnis died at the hands of vampires."

A scream rang out and chaos erupted. Geoffrey cried out several times for silence, and long minutes later, the mob settled down long enough to hear what he had to say. "Why did ye not report it to me, Andras?" Before he could answer, Geoffrey turned to Owen. "And why did ye confess to killing them?"

"We can discuss this in private, Geoffrey."

Andras's hard voice rang out over their heads. "Set Owen loose. Now, Tibbett."

"Aye, set the sin eater free," Sayer said his voice

hoarse with emotion. "He doesn't deserve to die by reason of his vocation. He's an innocent man."

"Mercy for the sin eater!" the widow Carnes shouted.

"Untie him," Mistress Hale echoed.

With a flick of his wrist, Geoffrey sliced through the hemp shackles. "Sorry, lad, 'twas doing my duty."

"What are we to do?" a panicked, female voice sobbed. "The undead have come to the shire."

Mimicking their mother's outcries of panic, children wailed, and men looked over their shoulders searching for the bloodthirsty enemy. Owen tore his gaze from Andras and looked down at Carys, touched by the tears sliding down her cheeks.

In the breath of a heartbeat the air grew thick with the shriek of banshees. What sounded like a thunderous flapping of wings overhead pierced the panicked voices of the crowd. Demonic guardians dipped, soared and hovered above them; their spines arched against a cloud-filled sky. Led by Dagan, the vampires descended, their arms open in graceful flight.

Cloaked in a pale mist of vapors, the vampire's crimson eyes blazed fire and their lethal white fangs dripped spittle. An odious stench drifted toward the gallows—a pungent mixture of ashes, the earth and death.

Owen assessed the scene. *Please, not Carys, don't take her.*

Dagan stood in the center of the paralyzed onlookers, his cape shimmering in a vibrant shade of blood red. Stunned into silence, villagers stared with their mouths agape, their eyes masked in terror.

Things happened so fast Owen couldn't remember their order. Dagan sliced through the throat of an innocent bystander with one swift slash of his hand. His companions rushed through the crowd, their dark clothing a wild haze of speed. So many were cut down while frozen in time; their legs anchored to the ground, the whites of their eyes the only part visible. Screams shook the stars, blood arced and streamed, and body parts soared through the air, heads, arms and legs. With vomit rising in his throat, Owen scanned the crowd for Carys and saw her brightly colored shawl. He jumped from the platform and shouted through the bedlam. "Run, Carys, run!"

Out of the corner of his eye, he saw Andras draw the sword and advance on a white-haired ghoul of ethereal beauty. Moving with speed and agility and striking faster than a viper, Andras cleaved an arm from the man's body. The demon reeled back with an anguished scream and pulled a claymore from the scabbard at his shoulder with his able hand.

The Prince's sword came up high, whirred through the air and keened its death knell. Sinking into the vampire's shoulder, the blade wobbled for a timeless moment before Andras pulled it free. The insufferable one fell back, but parried with a thrust toward Andras's heart. His dark eyes cold and lethal, Andras deflected the charge.

On and on it went, the long tooth striking, Andras parrying. Metal clanked and echoed across the bloody battlefield. Thunder rolled and lightning flashed in perfect sync with the warring steel. Time and again the blades met and clashed and Owen couldn't tear his eyes from the gruesome battle.

Until he heard Carys scream.

He looked in the direction of her voice and his knees knocked. Circling her, Dagan frothed at the mouth, his hands moving in slow motion to encase her throat.

Run, Owen, ye dolt, get to her before he kills her.

Without conscious thought, Owen lunged through

the air and executed a perfect landing on the vampire's back. He pummeled his fists into the hard muscle to no avail. Dagan flung him to the ground as if he weighed no more than a feather and resumed his advance on Carys.

Owen scrambled to his feet and stepped between them, his arms out at his sides, his voice cold. "Ye will have to kill me first to get to her."

"Sweet Mother of Jesus," Carys rasped behind him. "The hounds of Hell have arrived."

Crimson eyes flared. "I admit I'm baffled. I thought Andras was more your type." He cast an appreciative gaze on Carys. "Very well, your life for hers although I must say, she looks delectable."

Owen took a defensive stance and waited for the vampire to attack. Under his breath, he whispered, "Run, Carys. I saw Bellamy near the brick house."

Dagan's sinister laughter pierced the vapors shrouding him. "Oh be at ease; I'm not going to kill ye, handsome lad. I'm going to abduct ye."

Owen froze, and behind him Carys hadn't moved a muscle. He ripped the rope from his neck and passed it to her behind his back. "I said RUN, Carys!"

She bolted at the sound of his raised voice.

"Touching," Dagan said with a sneer. "Are ye coming peaceably or must I force ye?"

Praying for time until Andras could reach him, he attempted a stall. "Tell your black curs they're not to harm her."

The leader closed his eyes amid the destruction surrounding them and his body fell still. Several moments later, he opened them and looked at Owen. "Done. They'll not touch a hair on her head."

Owen glanced toward the ongoing battle with Andras and Dagan's man.

"Estevan will die, if that's what ye are wondering,

and your precious Maddock will live." He added, "For now."

Andras stared into the vampire's face and advanced. Pride swelled Owen's heart. More dazzling than the stars in heaven, he appeared as a surreal vision—his hair had come loose and fluttered behind him in the cool breeze of evening, and his clothing was in shreds from too many slices of vampire's sword. And yet he fought like the gallant, courageous man Owen had come to love.

He leaped high in the air, deflecting a vicious thrust from the ghoul. Landing on his feet seconds later, his hard features masked with strength and courage, he let loose the Prince's sword. Its cold steel hummed with infinite speed and accuracy.

A look of shock crossed the undead's face when the blade found a home in his forehead. The vampire's face shriveled like a prune, green liquid seeped from the wound and ran down his torso. He toppled to the ground, his death rasp echoing across the land as if coming from the belly of a large beast. Smoke billowed from his corpse; his limbs flailed about in the last throes of death and then stilled.

"See, did I not tell ye?"

Owen jerked his head back to Dagan and shriveled under the hypnotic glare.

"I allowed the girl to live; now ye must keep up your end of the bargain. I'm going to count to three. If ye haven't climbed upon my back by the time I'm done counting, I'll order my men to kill the lass ye are so fond of." His white gloves met when he clasped his hands. "One...two..."

Owen scrambled unto his back, took one last look at Andras and faster than the wind, the ground disappeared beneath him.

* * *

Clouds clung to the horizon in shades of gray and a ghastly black. Andras looked through the window in his study and thought about the senseless loss of life. The bagpipes would mourn for days, bonfires would blaze along the hillsides and salt and garlic would be placed on the stiles to keep the vampires from returning.

Guilt shrouded him. Would the folk have died if he'd surrendered the sword to Dagan? If he'd left Abergwaun after Traherne's attack, would his friends and neighbors have risen to a glorious morning today, gone about their simple lives in the usual manner?

He knew the answers to the questions. If he'd relinquished the Prince's sword, Dagan would have returned and exulted in the slaughter of innocent lives. Leaving Abergwaun might have stopped the killing here, but Dagan would have hunted him down and innocents from another village would have died.

One solution remained now...find Owen and kill Dagan so he could never prey on helpless humans again. He thought of Owen at the mercy of the vampire's wretchedness and ice spread through his veins. Mentally and physically engrossed in his battle with Estevan, he couldn't save Owen, and oh how the image of his lover's panic-stricken face haunted him now.

The long tooth's eyes had hardened into tiny shards of scarlet just before he took to the sky with Owen, an ominous warning meant for him alone. Andras knew what the demon was about—the sword for Owen's life. And Dagan would make him wait, bide his time until he was half-crazy with agony and desperation. He had to find Owen before Dagan infiltrated the lad's mind, before he.... Please, not that, anything but that.

It had taken hours last night to calm Carys after the carnage. He'd have to tell her this morning he'd be gone for most of the day searching for Owen. Where to look? What had he missed? He needed a sign, one little clue directing him to the vampire's lair.

And then the wrath of Duw would find them.

Chapter Fourteen

Against a lurid rising sun, the decaying turrets of a castle loomed ahead. Since he'd lost his sense of direction long ago, Owen had no idea which castle appeared in his line of vision.

A memory flooded his mind—the night Traherne almost killed him in the forest. He'd ridden through the night sky then on Andras's back, but the distance they'd traveled paled in comparison to the journey they took now.

Dagan soared with the dexterity of a hawk, or at least what Owen imagined the flight of a hawk to be. Despite the vampire's strength and expertise, his stomach roiled against the velocity and height as it had when he flew with Andras.

His transport landed in front of the massive structure with such elegance, it took Owen a fair amount of time to realize his feet had met solid ground again. With nausea swirling in the bowels of his belly and fear in his heart, he took in the full height and breadth of the frontage, hoping he'd recognize the abandoned edifice.

The castle rose up out of the ground at the end of a ridge, at a commanding crossing point of a river. To his right stood the remains of a three-story tower with columns of twelve-paned windows, and yet the adjoining tower to the left boasted Tudor-style windows in bad need of repair.

His eyes were drawn to the majestic cross guarding the entrance of the castle. Inlaid with fine Celtic knot-work and interlaced in a familiar ribbon pattern, it looked centuries old, yet had still maintained its reverence.

Turning his dizzy head, his gaze wandered to the porch and the lichen-ridden stones where the crests of

Henry VII, Arthur, Prince of Wales, and Arthur's wife, Catherine of Aragon were still visible. A memory of his father reading to him from one of the man's favorite history books nudged his memory, yet he couldn't place the name of the castle. How he wished now he'd paid more attention at the time.

The menacing half-laugh-half-snort Owen had come to recognize and hate came to him as a muffled echo. "I imagine it would harm none to divulge your whereabouts."

His queasiness abating, Owen's mind cleared. He'd forgotten Dagan had the capability of reading his thoughts. In the future, he'd be more careful about allowing his mind to wander when it came to anything the undead could use against him . . . or Andras. He shelved the troublesome thoughts entering his head about Andras lest Dagan pick them from his brain.

"Ye are standing before Carew Castle, once renowned as the most magnificent structure in all of south Wales. Pity it was abandoned in 1686." He narrowed his gaze and honed in on the façade. "What do ye make of the chapel? It's said when an Englishman arrives at a place, the first thing he builds is a store; when an American arrives at a new place, he builds a school, but when the Welsh settle, the very first thing they do is build a chapel." Dagan turned and faced him. "I visited several times when the castle stood in all its splendid glory, a benefit of traveling through time, of knowing the final part of a story where everything is made clear and no questions or surprises remain."

Having found a shred of his courage Owen felt his lips thin. "I care nothing about your past travels. No doubt ye preyed upon blameless folk then as ye do now."

When a red rim stamped his irises, Owen knew he'd roused Dagan's anger. Dagan advanced like the predator he was, his gait silent and reeking of stealth. "Let me remind ye, sin eater, I hold your life in my hands. The possibilities are endless and most are unpleasant." He leaned in, his mouth within inches of Owen's, the gossamer blue orbs studying every feature of his face. "Ye intrigue me. I don't believe I've seen a more stunning man throughout the centuries."

The absolute, emotionless inflection in his voice chilled Owen.

"What would it take, I wonder, to erase all memory of Maddock from your mind? I'm sure ye are aware he's not a pure blood. I like to refer to those who have been turned as halflings. While they possess a modicum of vampiric traits, the ability to shift into flying creatures for example, they lack the ability to travel through time. Did ye know our anatomy enables us to make use of our speed to escape predators? We have a well-developed sense of balance, a strong fight-or-flight instinct and...." He paused. "More importantly, we can read the thoughts of others. Ye'd do well to remember those traits if ye think to hinder my objectives."

While impaled by Dagan's steady gaze, Owen attempted to construct a wall around his soul. Andras's words reached his ears on the kiss of a breeze. "Ye must not allow it to happen, must fight it." Never had he found anything so difficult.

Dagan's hot breath whispered over him. "I can cut ye to shreds with one swipe of my hand or I can grant ye immortality. Together we can explore the universe, frolic in the distant past, and partake of every wicked sin known to man. Yield to me, Owen, and I promise ye a life unlike any ye have ever imagined."

Owen swallowed hard, the defiance in his voice seeming to come from another's lips.

"I'd rather die than yield to ye."

A flash of crimson spewed from Dagan's eyes,

almost blinding Owen. His hand came out, met his throat and he lifted him from the ground. "I should kill ye here and now, suck every drop of blood from your thankless veins."

Choking on the words, Owen managed to spit them out. "Ye will never possess your precious sword if ye kill me." Dagan released him and Owen gasped for air before addressing him again. "Maddock is no fool. He'll not surrender the claymore for a corpse."

"No," he said running his hands down the front of his cloak. "I don't imagine he would." The sun rose above the castle, its bright rays flooding the ground where they stood.

Dagan shrank back, pulled the hood of his cape over his long, dark locks and, with a flourish of his arm, motioned toward the decrepit front archway. "Your quarters await ye. I assure ye won't find them in the same base condition as the rest of the castle."

Owen walked toward the entry of the castle, gathering whatever control remained. He knew the chapter of this book had an ending. Like most events in life, if a man knew what was about to transpire, he'd find the means to cope. Fear of the unknown became his greatest enemy now, that and Dagan's unquenchable thirst for blood and killing.

Moments later, Dagan led him up several flights of stairs and along the dark and winding corridors until they stood before an entrance made of heavy stone. With a nod of the vampire's head, the door creaked and groaned, then opened.

Owen took in the spacious chamber. The aromas of incense, copper, and a briny smell that reminded him of the sea assailed his senses. Another spiraled up his nose after he digested the first three—an odor of sweet apples that had fallen from the tree and had begun to rot. He fought hard to keep the contents of his stomach where they belonged and drew a deep breath. On a more visceral level, the scents of suffering, desire and death washed over him, bringing him to his knees. At times like this, he loathed the heightened awareness bestowed upon him.

With sickening dread he scanned the area. No vermin-infested floors here. His eyes wandered to the hearth and to a pair Settle chairs with high, straight backs, complete with storage area. A trestle table of the finest oak graced the center of the room set with plates of silver and gold.

In the far corner of the room, an elaborate four poster bed with a headboard made of carved panels hugged a wall covered in rich, red silk. A tester of embroidered material had been strewn across the bed—as if whoever had used the covering last left in a rush—and above it, a matching valance caught his eye. Again his stomach heaved when he spied the heavy curtains draping the posts. They were meant to afford the occupants' privacy, but Owen didn't want to think about where *he* would be expected to retire.

Dispelling the sickening thought from his mind, he focused on a collection of war shields and Neolithic weapons adorning the fabric walls. Ominous-looking spears, polished stone hatchets and assorted armament sat in far corner of the room, the likes of which he'd seen only in his tad's picture books.

A shudder rippled down his spine with the realization he'd entered a long tooth's burrow, albeit one from the distant past.

"As ye can see, I'm a connoisseur of history. Having lived in many eras, it brings me comfort to live among familiar objects."

Caught up in a nightmare of the worst form, he realized Dagan was not only a blood- sucking vampire careless of all feeling but wrong in the noggin. To stir his anger would serve no one, least of all himself. Above all, he had to maintain a clear head and do the man's bidding until Andras found them. If Andras found them.

"I leave ye to your own devices until sunset." Dagan fixed him with a glare. "Ye will not be able to leave this chamber, other than to venture onto the balcony. I'd suggest ye also get some rest."

Still facing him, he took several steps back, turned and exited the chamber, though how he managed to walk through a wall eluded Owen. There seemed little sense in testing Dagan's theory about leaving the chamber after he'd just witnessed the man pass through a stone wall without so much as flinching. If he could conjure these quarters, he could call forth invisible barriers.

Owen walked onto the balcony and stared at the magnificent view, the rolling acres of lush green hills and the pristine waters of the mill pond. Hadn't he read somewhere that vampires feared water and would not cross under any circumstances? So why had he chosen Carew Castle with its acreage of endless water guarding the frontage? Did he think Andras would not dare venture across it should he find them, or had Dagan developed immunity to the aqua depths? Owen expelled a lungful of air; so many questions with few answers.

His gallant prince would come for him, he felt it with his every breath, but would it be too late?

* * *

Night embraced the stars as Andras stumbled toward the yellow mouth of the cave. Weakened by mind-numbing fatigue after searching for three days, he dropped to the ground with a moan of disappointment and rage.

His options were exhausted. He'd looked high and low for any trace of the vampire's lair without success.

Closing his eyes, he prayed the land of forgetfulness would claim him.

From the deepest vault of his mind, Andras dreamed of Traherne, vine-cloaked forests and black-winged creatures. And he dreamed of Halwn, Owen's father. Compassionate, green eyes looked down on him and gentle hands lifted his broken body onto a forage wagon meant to haul garden fare.

"I can't take ye to my abode; I wouldn't know how to explain it to my son," he'd said. "I'll harbor ye in a farmhouse that hasn't heard the sound of a human voice for years."

In his dreams he saw Halwn place food, water and a mixture of herbs near his cot, claiming the pungent remedy would draw out the fever and help mend his wounds. An image of him searching through his medical journals entered his dreams. He discovered the grave injuries healed at an accelerated rate of their own volition and he found out why. It seemed vampires possessed a number of attributes humans lacked—excessive speed, the ability to take to the sky, and a rapid mending of injuries fatal to mankind.

His worst fears were confirmed between the pages of those reports. While he knew in his heart a long tooth had set upon him, he couldn't face it in those first days after the attack. When he began to develop an unquenchable thirst and his thoughts lingered for hours about hunting down beasts in the woods, he could no longer deny the truth.

Owen appeared among the montage of images rushing through his sleep-drugged brain, as he appeared the first time Andras had laid eyes on him and the last time he looked upon his face. In the first version, laughter bracketed his generous mouth. In the final image his eyes flared with hopelessness and fear.

Halwn appeared again, the vision so disturbing,

Andras felt the blood rush to his head. The man put his arms around Owen's shoulder, led him away, and they disappeared into the pale, gray mist. Excruciating agony, like a knife twisting in his gut, found him in the dream world. What did it mean? Had Owen died, or was he about to die and join his tad in Duw's kingdom? Would he never again languish in the blissful world Owen had taken him to, inhale the fresh, clean scent of his burnished locks, or taste the exquisite lips?

Just when Andras thought all hope lost, Halwn stopped and turned to him. His outstretched arm beckoned him. "Come," he said. "I'll show ye where the ambrosia of your soul is."

Andras jackknifed up from the hard, cold floor of the cavern, his brow dripping sweat, his pulse racing. He looked toward the mouth of the cave and saw twilight had come to the land. The wind keened through the trees, carrying the old sin eater's voice, again saying, "Come, I'll show ye where the ambrosia of your soul is."

He plucked his sword from the ground and raced toward the entrance of the cave, and then onward to the coastline below. Andras saw nothing but the black rocks rising up out of the sea-green depths, heard only the foaming roll of the ocean and the lonesome cry of the birds circling overhead.

"'Twas just a dream, no more," he said fighting the curtain of desolation shrouding him. "Why did ye appear, Halwn? Must ye also torment me?"

A hazy mirage of the old sin eater appeared. The familiar mark of the crow stamped the corners of his eyes and a smile stretched his lips. Halwn motioned him forward. Andras sprinted along the sandy shore, the Prince's sword slapping against his thigh. Long minutes later and wheezing from his efforts, he realized he'd never catch the vision; for every step he put behind him, Halwn buried two.

When the old man disappeared amid a blue fog, a bellow of misery spewed from his throat. Dejected, he came to an abrupt halt and dropped his chin to his chest. There at his feet, a sketch materialized in the sand. He fell to his knees, studied it, and threw up his hands in a gesture of gratitude. A far cry from the portrait of a castle hanging in the great hall of his manor home, a crude etching rose up to meet him. "Carew Castle," he uttered to the vacant air. A mixture of emotions flooded him—elation, rage and fear. His search for Owen had ended.

His descent into Dagan's Shadowland of Hell had just begun.

Chapter Fifteen

Seated by the hearth and playing a fiddle that happened to appear that morning, Owen heard Dagan enter the chamber. The vampire walked to the altar, recited a series of arcane incantations—in Latin—and joined him near the fire.

Tonight, his eyes were more cerulean than deep cobalt, but hypnotic nonetheless. With too much time on his hands to think, Owen spent hours that day trying to recollect the passages from *Lords of the Underworld: Vampyres*. How naïve he'd been while searching through the book, his only intention at the time to confirm or refute his suspicions about Andras, nothing more. Yet here he was, captive of the vilest undead Diawl ever breathed life into. Dagan lived up to the book's portrayal of vampyres. His lair screamed luxurious fabrics and rich scents, and one passage in the book indicated vampyres were hypnotic creatures who possessed charismatic traits and seductive powers. All of the above fit Dagan, and Owen couldn't remember a time in his life when he'd been so terrified.

The decadent mouth spoke to him. "Ye found the fiddle I left for ye."

"Thank ye," Owen managed to reply without looking at him.

Dagan wouldn't allow his slight to pass. He leaned in and, placing his elbows on his knees, rested his chin in his palms. "Ye don't fear me, do ye?"

"My life has value as long as Andras has the sword."

"Yes, but don't delude yourself. Soon the Prince's claymore will be in my possession."

His stare drilled into him. "What will your life be worth then?"

"What will yours be worth when Andras comes for

ye?" He knew his life hung in the balance and only one thing kept him alive—Dagan's unquenchable yearning to own the sword.

Laughter shook the overhead beams. "Ye do intrigue me, Owen." His tone took on a hard edge. "Look at me when I speak to ye!"

Owen lifted his chin and met his eyes, mindful to resist with every ounce of power he could summon.

"I can do whatever I wish with ye." Slender, white fingers reached out and brushed his cheek. "Make ye submit to my sexual desires. I could kill ye should the mood strike me, or make ye mine for all eternity."

"Or ye could continue to torment me."

"Oh, my sweet lad, I don't mean to torment ye."

A vague haziness took over his senses. *Resist, Owen, ye must resist his power.*

"Given the three choices, which would ye choose?"

He struggled with uncertainty, the drone of his compelling voice seeping into his brain. *Do not yield, do not allow him in.* Seething with contempt for Dagan and all of his kind, the words rushed forth. "I'd choose the second; I would rather die than submit or belong to ye for all eternity."

Quicker than he could draw a breath, a vise-like grip tightened about his throat. Dagan lifted him from the chair until his feet dangled in mid-air. His face blue with rage, the vampire stared into his eyes. "Don't ever challenge me again."

He struggled for air; knew he'd pushed Dagan too far this time. The room began to fade before him, dancing in myriad shades of silver, gold and blue. . . always the blue, blue eyes. Just when he thought he'd breathed his last, Dagan released some of the pressure, allowing a tiny squeak of air to enter.

Lust replaced the anger in Dagan's eyes. White fangs emerged and his mouth descended toward his neck. Owen closed his eyes and called forth every scrap of courage within his reservoir. Willing his voice to calm, he said the first thing that came to his mind. "Andras will not hand over the sword if ye damn me. He doesn't walk the path of the insufferable ones, and will have no use for me if ye relegate me to such a life."

Dagan's ravenous hunger, like a living breathing entity coiled around them, cocooned them in a tangled labyrinth of white-hot passion Owen thought might kill him. Like an addict who can't resist the opium, the long tooth's allure was so potent, for a moment he longed to surrender.

His words must have struck a dissonant chord. Dagan released the grip on his neck and he crashed to the floor in a heap. Gasping for air, he realized how close he came to being undead. Dagan looked down on him for a long time without saying a word, pivoted, and walked away.

He curled up into a ball to control his tremors and wondered how long he could deny the vampire's overpowering enchantment.

* * *

Dagan watched the dark sky cling to the misty moors of Carew Castle. Bonfires set by his own hand hissed and sputtered on the hillsides, lighting the path for the hag he was about to call forth.

Darksome night and shining moon, Hearken to the witches' rune.

East then South, West then North, Hear! Come! I call thee forth!

With a loud whoop the Gwrach sprang through the bracken and planted her stooped body before him. Bone thin, her tattered clothing worn clean through, bloodshot eyes raked him over. A wild tangle of white hair framed her sharp features—hooked nose, pointed teeth and pencil-thin lips. Behind her stood a league of her servants, zombies willing and able to do her bidding at the crook of her spiny finger.

Unfazed by her imposing presence, Dagan looked down his nose and returned her discerning stare. "What is the name of the hag I have summoned forth?"

"The coin," she said extending her hand.

With a roll of his eyes, he dug into the pocket of his brocade vest and placed a leather pouch into her palm.

"Hester Potts of Wrexham, my Lord."

"From the trials held in Chester, 1656?"

"Aye, the same."

"Bradshaw hung three witches at Boughton Chester and a fourth escaped into the nearby woods, never to be heard from again."

A hair-raising cackle snapped the air. "'Twas lucky for me the hounds lost my scent." The hag cocked her head and looked into his eyes. "My Lord didn't summon me to engage in idle banter about witch trials."

"No, I summoned ye to cast a spell. What assurance do I have ye are a Black Witch?"

A lopsided grin transformed her craggy features. "The White Witches would think it beneath them to cavort with ghouls."

He glanced over her shoulder for a second look at her companions. "Yes, I imagine they would."

"What is the nature of the spell ye seek?"

He rocked back on his heels, weighing his words before he spoke. "It's of a delicate nature."

"Speak. I cannot assist if I don't know the nature of the quandary."

"Very well. There's a sin eater in my midst, one possessed with the sight. I'm unable to penetrate his thoughts." He snorted. "Much less control them."

She flinched before her chilling shriek rent the air. "Ai! Ai! Yeeeee! A sin eater, ye say?"

They exchanged a long, deep look before Dagan's

cold voice froze the air between them. "Return the coin. I'll summon a Gwrach worth the weight of the pouch." The zombies stirred behind her, held in check by the hag's raised hand.

She closed her eyes. "Permit me to channel the oracle." Long minutes passed and then she opened her eyes, the wolfish shadow of her face stark white against the burning embers of the bonfires, defining the strains of evil embracing her. "The sin eater's powers are strong, woven throughout the centuries with unbreakable threads."

"It's ye who must speak freely now."

"'Tis folly the folk embrace in deeming sin eaters unholy. The man ye covet is a Dyn Hysbys."

Advancing on the hag, Dagan felt his fangs descend. "Ye lie! The lad is no wizard, but a simple man."

Low-pitched growls heaved the stagnant air, and again she checked her demonic army with a silent command of her gnarled hand. "He descends from a line of spirits who came before mankind. The very name Owen means *born well*." Spittle oozed from her lips. "Think, My Lord, do not all sin eaters live at the edge of the forest, at the boundary between light and dark, good and evil?"

"Because they are shunned by their own kind, feared for the sins they have ingested."

"'Tis a false belief, held by those who also believe if a child is born under a new moon, it will grow up to be eloquent of speech. Dribble, superstitious babble, nothing more, My Lord."

"Tell me of his powers and if ye play me false, I'll hunt ye down and tear out your miserable throat."

She hesitated and looked toward the pocket of his vest. With another roll of his eyes, Dagan reached inside and delivered an additional pouch to her hand.

"He has the power to exorcise spirits and ghosts, cure disease and lift curses by means of the cross and the Trinity. The clergy despise their kind, not only because the folk have chosen their services over the deliverance of the Last Rites, but they succeed where the holy men fail in exorcising evil spirits."

He loomed over her, the odious stench of her person choking him. "Ye will conjure a spell, divest him of these powers and in the process erase all memory from his mind."

"'Tis an insurmountable bidding."

"Do it or no longer will ye wander the woods of Wrexham!" Caught up in the maelstrom of fury, Dagan's red cape billowed around him.

"As ye wish, Sire."

She closed her eyes and moments later, the bonfires spit and flared, the heavens shifted and lightning pierced the sky. Impressed with her black magick skills, Dagan's anger receded and wanton desire took flight in the pit of his groin.

"'Tis done," she said her eyes blazing amber fire.

"Be gone from my sight and take your wretched flesh-eating ghouls with ye."

In the distance, the woeful howl of a wolf pierced the night sky. Dagan staggered back and searched the surrounding terrain amid the hag's ear-splitting screech. "They come!" she said, shrinking. "The lycans are upon ye!"

His disdain for the Gwach laced his words. "Ye shrivel like a coward beneath the wolf's cry."

"Nay, not just any wolf, my Lord."

His gaze roamed the fog-shrouded moors, his eyes narrowing under the foreboding undercurrents enveloping them.

Her voice taut with fear, her rheumy eyes darker than thunderclouds, she spat the words. "Ye shouldn't have allowed your clan to desecrate their graves near Pembroke Castle."

He whirled to stare at her, his temper rising. "Stave them off until my business is concluded here. Sic your army of zombies upon them."

Her eyes sought the pocket of his vest. "'Tis a large army I lead, with many needs."

This time, Dagan didn't drop the pouch into her palm, but tossed it at her feet. "The pouch holds twice the coin of the others. I'll need a powerful charm to defeat the Prince of Wales's sword."

She bowed her white head. "As ye wish, my Lord."

"Now leave me, lest I forget my manners."

Her lips moved in silent chant and then the Gwach and her legions disappeared like smoke rising above the treetops. Dagan conjured a bevy of timber for the blazing bonfires—a strong deterrent against werewolves—turned on his heels and headed toward the entrance of the castle.

Visions of the lad with hair the color of autumn leaves and features carved by a skilled stone mason flooded him. He couldn't surrender him now, wouldn't. Maddock would come for the sin eater. When he did, he'd finish where his father left off. Soon the revered claymore would be his, and so would Owen Rhys...through all eternity.

Dagan stepped into the dank bowels of the castle and headed for the chamber.

* * *

Unfamiliar sounds seeped into the bedchamber, rousing Owen from a fitful sleep. Overhead, a tapestry valance striated with narrow bands of silver and gold crowned the four-poster bed, and beneath him, sheets of the finest linen brushed against his bare torso.

Wallowing in a cesspool of ambiguity, he clutched the luxurious coverlet to his chin, drew himself up and glanced over his shoulder. A red-caped man stood before an altar, and three more knelt before him, their bowed heads gleaming under the flames of filigree candelabra. An eerie chant filled the room, the words spoken in an ancient language he couldn't begin to decipher.

He shook his dulled brain in an attempt to dislodge the bizarre thoughts entering. *Ye must fight it.* He'd heard the words somewhere, but couldn't place the source. The somnolent voice from across the room mesmerized him, pitched him into a world of erotic fantasies he had no desire to leave.

He reached deep into the recesses of his mind for a recollection from his past, any scrap to tell him where he'd come from and how he'd arrived here. While floundering in confusion, the fall of footsteps coming toward him sent his heart into a tremulous beat.

The man's beauty bedeviled him. Dark waves framed his flawless, pale skin and timeless features. Vibrant, sea-kissed eyes drew him like an ill-fated moth seeking the fiery flames of death. *Ye must not allow it to happen; ye must fight it.* Ah, but he didn't want to fight against this potent magick; he wanted to submit, surrender to the overpowering glamour summoning him.

A slender hand, bejeweled with sparkling stones, reached out for him. "Ye see, three days have passed and no harm has found ye. Yield to me now, Owen, and I promise ye a life unlike any ye have ever imagined."

Owen. His name was Owen. Then who was this dazzling being asking him to yield? He came to his feet and took the offered hand, spellbound by the hypnotic eyes—eyes he'd seen in another time and place, though where and when he no longer knew. The man leaned down, his eyes blazing with an odd mixture of lust and another expression he knew so well...death.

Hot, primal arousal drifted over him, around him, stealing whatever resistance he intended to summon. At the moment, he'd do anything the man required of him. The stranger's ravenous gaze peered through the window of his soul and robbed him of sane thought. With fangs bared, his head descended and burrowed into Owen's neck. He should fight. Hadn't someone told him to fight?

A scream filled the room, followed by a rush of pain so intense his hands dug into the man's hard shoulders. The smell of blood wafted around him—rich and thick with a faint trace of copper. A euphoric surge rushed through his veins, so powerful he wondered what he'd done to deserve Gwyddon Ecstasy. His heart tattooed a fragile beat, a mere whisper of its once steady rhythm. Flaccid limbs buckled beneath him, the essence of his soul bid him farewell and journeyed toward his swollen tongue. Soon it would escape through his mouth and disappear like dust. This was the reason he'd seen death. He'd prophesied his own demise.

Strong arms cradled him and carried him to the bed, the honeyed timbre of the man's voice placing him into a catatonic state. "Mine," he rasped. "All mine through eternity."

Accepting his fate, the man called Owen closed his eyes and walked into the demonic realms of Hell.

Chapter Sixteen

His path drawn by a primordial map of pale white stars, Andras soared through the sky with an image of Owen's face etched on his brain. He couldn't think about what had transpired during the three days Owen had been ensnared in Dagan's insidious clutches; he had to concentrate on the single goal of freeing him.

The crumbling towers of Carew Castle came into view below him. He circled the massive structure and noticed only one turret that wasn't exposed to the open sky. Decades of harsh elements had eroded the exterior and interior, like so many of the ghostlike castles dotting the Welsh landscape.

Against a boom of thunder, Andras landed on his feet near the gatehouse. The air hissed with menacing undercurrents, and around him the enormous trunks of the yews groaned as if warning him the wrath of Hell was about to unfurl.

He checked his weapons—the Prince's sword holstered in the scabbard about his waist and the twin dirks he'd stuffed into his high leather boots. The daggers would do little to keep Dagan at bay, but perhaps they'd serve as a distraction in a crucial moment.

One long tooth had met his fate during the battle at Abergwaun, which meant four of Dagan's minions still lived to wreak havoc on the unfortunate. If he had his druthers, all would die tonight by his blade. A long shot, he knew, but he kept repeating the words "Die by my blade" while creeping along the algae-riddled wall of the barbican. With Duw, all things were possible.

"Who goes there?" a voice rang out, quaking with panic.

Why would one of Dagan's demons tremble over

his expected arrival? While they should fear Glyndŵr's claymore, five against one were fair odds...in their favor. With little time to ponder the reason for the man's apprehension, Andras picked up a hefty stone at his feet and tossed it into the night. Seconds later, a loud clank against the metal gait echoed in his ears. As expected, the long tooth stepped out from his barricade to investigate while Andras slipped through the deteriorating archway over the entry.

The walls of the structure vibrated when a snap of lightning cracked the air. On the heels of the unexpected flash, a section of limestone splintered from the ceiling, missing Andras's head by inches. A close call, no doubt a prelude of what awaited him.

Drawing on a memory of long ago, he closed his eyes and imagined the layout of the castle in daylight through the eyes of a ten-year old boy. Uncle Maxen's penchant for archeology had brought them to the doorstep of many abandoned historical haunts. If recollection served him, the northwest tower resided at the end of the winding staircase. He tamped down the surge of fear rising up from his gut; not fear of losing his life, but raw-edged terror over Owen's fate at the hands of Dagan. He found it hard not to imagine the worst: Owen becoming an object of Dagan's lustful desires or worse, an object of his bloodthirsty cravings. He embraced the fear; in fact, sheer black panic propelled him up the stairs.

A door loomed ahead, the only possible entrance to the interior of the tower. A resonant chant filtered through a tiny crack in the wall, so minuscule, he wondered how the ancient mantra had slipped through.

Another sound found him, the demonic howls of wolves along the moors. The hair at the nape of his neck and forearms stood at attention. Another possible hindrance he didn't have time to think about now. He checked his weapons one last time and when the door burst open, he decided someone from above must be watching over him. A trio of long tooths sped by—without bothering to look left or right—their red eyes glowing like burning embers, their jaguar-like incisors gleaming against the torches in their hands. In a blur of motion they clambered down the steps as if Cŵn Annwn, the spectral black hounds of The Otherworld, chased their heels.

Werewolves had come to Carew Castle. He smelled their fetid odor, sensed their presence. Duw spare him the added misery. Of all times, why had the lycanthropes chosen this night to battle the long tooth?

The door to the chamber stood ajar. He pushed it open with his toe and stepped into the candlelit room. Two men stood at an altar, their cloaked heads bowed, their lips moving as they recited the archaic incantation. One looked up, trapped his gaze and held it. Andras's heart plummeted to his feet.

Owen.

"Welcome to our provisional abode, Maddock." Dagan stretched out his arms, palms up, without raising his head. "We've been waiting your arrival. Haven't we, Owen?"

Owen didn't respond, but stared straight ahead, not even an eyelash flutter, a tic of his lip, nothing. A dull knife sliced through Andras's heart and his stomach heaved. Please, not that, anything but that. "Owen, what has he done to ye?"

A mere shell of his former self, glazed eyes—absent a shred of recognition—looked into Andras's. His bloodless skin contrasted against the black hood covering his nut- brown hair, and for a moment Owen teetered, as if the slightest flare from the candelabra gracing the altar would send him toppling to the floor.

The vampire tossed his head back, his insidious

laughter shattering the eerie stillness. "Ye are too late, Maddock. Your lover doesn't recognize ye, remembers nothing of his past life—not your touch or the whisper of his name on your lips. Pity that."

Blind rage oozed from every pore in Andras's body. "I'll take ye apart limb by limb before I sever your head from your neck."

The long tooth emerged from the altar, all billowy red robe and fiery eyes. "Ye can try, although I doubt the Prince's sword can withstand my magick now. Why don't we make this simple—ye hand over the claymore in exchange for the sin eater?"

"Not on your black heart."

"Very well." Dagan sloughed his cloak with a flick of his wrist and pulled a rapier from a scabbard around his shoulder. "Don't say I didn't warn ye."

Steel blades flashed in the candlelit room. Andras advanced on Dagan's right, taunting him with the razor-sharp tip. "Come, arch demon of Satan, taste the kiss of death."

* * *

Watching the macabre scene playing out before him, Owen gripped the edge of the altar until his knuckles turned white. He had to remember what brought him here. For what ungodly reason was he standing before Lucifer's dais bearing witness to a fight to the death between vampires?

Long, white fangs descended, first Dagan's and then the stranger's. The intruder moved with practiced skill, taunting Dagan with several quick jabs to his silk shirt. Anger flashed in his leader's eyes before he hurled a fireball toward the stranger with an agile flick of his wrist. The man deflected it with his blade and sent it hurling toward the gold ceiling overhead.

Who was this black-hearted killer?

"Touché, Maddock." Dagan bowed at the waist.

"Well done."

Maddock? A ripple of unease passed over Owen. Why did the name ring familiar?

From above, a triangle of light shadowed the man's handsome face. Gray eyes sparked a flash of crimson before the man lunged, his magnificent weapon slicing through Dagan's forearm.

A scream tore from the leader's throat. He reeled back and clutched his arm. "May ye rot in Lucifer's kingdom for all eternity!"

Dagan's eyes hardened into tiny shards of scarlet. Like a viper he struck, fast and deadly, before carving out a deep gash in the stranger's thigh. The man staggered back, but regained his footing and countered with a strike of his own. Metal clanked as their swords crossed, to part and meet again seconds later. Mesmerized by the frenetic motion of parry and thrust, retreat and advance, Owen couldn't tear his gaze from the macabre scene. Moments later, they separated, their chests heaving, their ragged breaths scattering like icy vapors.

Dagan's emotionless tone cut through the noxious air of the chamber. "Why don't ye tell your lover what lies in wait for him? Tell him how it feels to live day after day thirsting for human blood, craving it with every cell in your body. I wonder, will he also deny himself the pleasure of drinking the purest elixir known to man or beast?"

"Ye must fight it, Owen, mustn't allow it to happen." The intruder spoke, his voice steadfast and sure.

Like an old wound that festered, awareness seeped into his beleaguered brain. A tiny fleck of knowledge took root, twisting and turning through his gut like a serpent. He should know those words, that voice, the familiar spellbinding eyes.

"How prosaic," Dagan said. "I've a few parting words of my own for ye, Andras."

"Andras." The word fell from Owen's lips like a reverent invocation.

"Soon I'll finish the job Traherne started. How foolish of my sire to allow ye to bleed out in the forest. Rest assured I won't make the same mistake."

Owen's brain shifted, struggling to summon the familiar names. *Traherne?*

"We could have had the Prince's sword in our possession long ago were it not for his lack of foresight. In his defense, he had no way of knowing the old sin eater would happen across ye and save your sorry carcass. Imagine that, the greatest vampire in the world fucked up."

Sin Eater? Owen released an audible gasp when the screams of banshees rushed through the open window. In the span of a heartbeat, the stranger dropped his guard, his gray eyes piercing the distance between them. A fleeting play of emotion crossed his features—compassion, pride and love.

A grave mistake on the stranger's part. He should have kept his amazing eyes on Dagan. The fierce vampire brought his sword up high, and on the downswing, buried the hilt in the man called Maddock's shoulder. He crumbled to his knees, yanked the steel blade from his flesh, and tossed it across the room.

The shock of the man's impending defeat held Owen immobile.

"I'm disappointed in your precious sword's performance, Maddock. And yours."

The stranger rose with great effort and struck what would have normally been a fatal blow, but the vampire's magick protected him. Like an invisible shield, an incendiary circle of fire enveloped him, an impregnable barrier the gem-hilted sword couldn't penetrate. Pulling a pair of daggers from his boots, the stranger hurled them through the air. Hitting the swirling mass of dust and vapors at its heart, the knives bounced off the defensive wall and clanked to the floor with a dull thud.

A relentless succession of fireballs streaked through the space separating their bodies, pummeling the shiny blade and the stranger's hand. The smell of seared flesh filled the chamber as the rapier flew from the man's grasp and landed in a deafening clatter near the altar. The stranger fell to the floor, gasping for breath, clutching his injured hand.

Dagan advanced with a glazed look of imminent victory. "The time has come to end this pitiful game of cat and mouse." He placed a foot on the man's chest. "And alas, I lied. I acquire the sword and the sin eater. Take one last look at your lover's face, Andras, because now ye ride straight into the gates of Hell!"

"No, ye do, Dagan!" Owen shouted from across the room.

The vampire whirled around, his face a mask of shock as he faced Owen. His hands moved in frenetic motion to conjure another spell, but Owen dispelled each and every charm he called forth with the newfound power of his mind.

"Owen, wait!" Dagan's hands went still and rested near his hips, palms up. "I've promised ye a life of immortality, eternity." His voice took on the innocent pleadings of a child.

Owen hurled the sword with the speed of a comet racing through the night sky, severing Dagan's head from his body. "This is the only eternity ye will ever see."

* * *

Andras clawed his way across the floor, fangs bared and a bestial growl rolling from his gut. He covered Dagan's body with his and dove for his neck. Stunned by the events he'd witnessed and the burgeoning surge of power he felt, precious seconds lapsed before Owen closed the distance and yanked Andras from his body. "Cease! Don't do it!"

Andras turned to look at him. His crimson eyes glossed over, his fangs dripping saliva. "Turn me loose!"

He yanked with all his might. "Andras, ye are no better than him if ye proceed. I beseech ye. It's what Dagan longed for, what his sire wanted, for ye to become like them, surrender to your cravings." He fell upon him and cradled his head. "Ye once told me 'tis the only thing ye have left."

"I no longer care. Let go of me! I'll suck every drop of blood from his wretched body."

Assailed by a terrible sense of hopelessness, Owen released him and watched Dagan's soul slip from his mouth. The mist wasn't gray, but black; and it didn't spiral upward, but downward into the bowels of Hell. Desolation tinged his voice. "Then I'll join ye. If this is the life ye choose after all this, I choose it too."

"Nay!"

"Aye, I go where ye go now. If ye become the beast, so must I."

Owen lowered his head into his hands and waited for the coppery smell of blood to fill his senses. So much senseless killing, and for what? Long minutes passed before he lifted his chin and looked into Andras's eyes. "What are ye waiting for?"

"I found what I was waiting for."

"Tell me, what is it?"

"For someone to knock some sense into my thick noggin, show me the true path." He ran his hand down the silky hair at the side of Owen's head. "Forgive me."

"There is nothing to forgive, Andras. Mayhap the time will come when ye are forced to do the same for me."

"Duw help us now."

A series of demonic howls drifted through the castle walls, followed by the terrifying screams of dying men.

"Werewolves," Andras said.

"I heard Dagan say they desecrated their graves near Pembroke Castle."

"Perhaps he'll have the last laugh yet."

Owen glanced toward the door of the chamber. "What will happen?"

"As soon as they've finished tearing Dagan's men apart, they'll come for us. They don't care who disturbed their graves once they embark down a path of revenge and bloodlust. Put the sword in my hand. Perhaps it still retains a bit of its powers."

Owen took his good hand and wrapped it around the hilt of the Prince's claymore.

"Nine shames on that miserable cur! He cast a spell on my weapon as well."

"Ye are in no condition to fight werewolves even if your sword wasn't possessed."

"What do ye propose we do, lie here and wait for the jaws of death to tear us to pieces?"

"Can ye walk, Andras?"

"I'm not sure. Whatever magick he conjured arrived with a charm that prevents healing. Where would we go in any event?"

"To the water."

"'Tis not vampires we must elude, but lycanthropes."

"Some believe werewolves transform into long tooths after death. If a vampire will not cross the water, perhaps the same can be said of the lycanthrope."

Andras reached up and touched his face. "'Tis a grand idea. Go, Owen, and save yourself. I'll wait here and do my best to hinder their progress, at least until ye make it to the river in front of the castle."

"Get up, Andras! I'll not leave ye so unless ye want to see them rip me limb-from-limb, get your mangy carcass off this floor."

He closed his eyes and drew a tired breath. "My thigh is cut clear through to the bone and the same could be said about my shoulder. There are no words to describe the pain in my hand. Hurry now, there is little time."

"Very well, ye leave me no choice. So far I've done little to tarnish my good name; I never thought to see the day I'd resort to the Diawl's hoodoo."

A pained smile parted Andras's lips. "Not all magick is the devil's work."

"Stop blabbering whilst I concentrate. Casting spells and charms is a novel concept to me."

"I'm confident ye will acquire the gist of it fairly soon."

"Andras, please."

He closed his eyes again with a groan and Owen did the same, minus the protracted moan. His lips moved, the words tumbling forth foreign to his ears. The room spun overhead and the domed ceiling faded away and opened to an ebony sky complete with a hard-driven rain. Thigh-deep water swirled around them, the sound of waves in the distance roaring as if sent by the hand of some mystical being Owen didn't want to know the name of. He clutched Andras's jerkin to keep his head above the water and struggled to remain on his feet.

Near the gate, the remains of Dagan's men flashed beneath a stream of lightning shot from the sky. Thunder rolled overhead but not loud enough to drown out the wild fearsome yowls of the werewolves as they advanced.

On a full run toward the mill pond, their yellow eyes glowed feral and spiked teeth gnashed at the vacant air. Owen swallowed the fear in his throat. Not like this; he couldn't bear to see Andras ripped apart by the wolves.

In desperation with all hope lost, he recited the only words that came to his benumbed mind, words his tad taught him long ago. "I give easement and rest now to thee, troubled souls. Come not down the lanes or in our meadows. And for thy peace, I pawn my own soul. Amen."

The demons came to an abrupt halt at the edge of the water, their frantic howls rising above the wailing wind and pelting rain.

"I give easement and rest now to thee, troubled souls!" he shouted. "Come not down the lanes or in our meadows. And for thy peace, I pawn my own soul. Amen."

The shrill barks echoed across the turbulent water and then faded to guttural snarls.

"I consume your earthly transgressions, weary travelers, and render your sinless souls free. For your peace, I pledge my own soul. Amen!" Owen raised his hand in the air. "Amen, go in peace!" As if baffled by the strange creature shouting across the blue depths of the water separating them, the werewolves took several steps back. A moment of time passed in which Owen held his breath. Releasing it a long time later, his words drifted across the tumultuous waves. "Go in peace!"

One by one they retreated, turned and dashed across the rain-shrouded moors, their howls fading with every passing minute.

"They fear your powerful magic, sin eater." Andras clutched his chest, his hoarse cough scattering amid the frothy tides of the pond.

"As do I," he said hauling Andras toward shore

foot by painstaking foot. A long time later, Owen collapsed on the sandy beach beside Andras. "I've no idea how to transport us home from here."

"Home," Andras whispered. "Too much time has passed since I've thought about my ancestral home." He smiled up at Owen through the pouring rain. "Give me a moment to gather my strength."

"Take all the time ye require, but how far is it we must travel?"

"By means of foot or by way of the crow?"

"Tell me both so I might choose the mode."

"'Tis a full days' walk to Abergwaun; but a blink of an eye for the crow."

Owen groaned and clutched his stomach. "'Tis a good thing I've not eaten in days."

A chuckle left Andras's lips.

Owen looked at him askance. "What amuses ye so amid a cauldron of supernatural travails?"

"The thought of my Uncle Maxen."

"'Tis daft ye are. I think Dagan seared your brain rather than your hand."

"Ye will understand once ye meet him."

The rain stopped and a prolonged silence fell between them. Wet and soaked through to the skin, Owen couldn't stop trembling. Or was it Andras's words that had pitched his body into hopeful tremors? He asked the question as if testing his hearing. "Will I meet him?"

"Aye, just as soon as I can get us out of here and gather Carys and Bellamy." Another laugh fell from his lips, followed by a chortled cough. "Then ye will rue the day ye ever laid eyes on the peculiar man."

Chapter Seventeen

Andras's elegant manor house resided on the crest of heather-riddled hillock several rods from where Sycharth Castle once stood. Owen fell in love with the land and the people who occupied it after arriving a fortnight ago.

Andras's Uncle Maxen lived up to his reputation as a foppish dandy. The man's waistcoats and cravats were woven from the finest quality fabrics, befitting a jester of his status, and not once since Owen's arrival had the man appeared in public without his stove-pipe hat and walking cane. Engrossed in *The Poetical Works of Thomas Gray*, Maxen could recite from memory a repertoire of bon mots and quatrains that launched Owen into a perpetual state of belly-laughs.

Carys kept him company throughout the day, and if she had other tasks to occupy her, he passed his time rambling around the massive structure. Whether immersed in one of many books from the library's vast collection or squandering his hours in the enormous kitchen sampling Cook's delectable fare, the time had passed quickly since arriving here. His nights, however, were a different matter altogether.

This morning, Andras found him in the library while pondering the dark stirrings that had entered his life. Owen's skin tingled when the powerful presence crossed the parquet flooring and slithered—he could think of no other word for it—into a chair opposite him near the hearth.

The flint-honed gaze studied him for a lengthy time before he spoke. Andras seldom asked folk to accommodate him; the man excelled at cutting to the heart of the matter. "Tell me what troubles ye so."

"Nothing to be concerned about. I'm a bit overwhelmed at times with the opulence, the elegance."

Owen scanned the room. "'Tis hard for me reconcile my humble origins against so much wealth."

"One grows accustomed to it in time, but one should never forget from whence he came." Owen watched his face grow still and his expression turn serious. "'Tis more than that. Have ye forgotten I've been where ye are now?"

He shook his head. "Would be hard for anyone to forget such a thing."

Andras studied his face. "Are ye discontented here, displeased with me in—"

"Nay! Don't think it."

"There must be truth and frank candor between us. I can't diminish your misery unless ye speak your heart."

His mind congested with doubt and fear, Owen looked away. "I know not where to begin."

"Where one must always begin; at the source of the blackness."

He closed his eyes against the desolation sweeping over him, the silence lengthening.

"Quid pro quo, how about that?"

"I'm unfamiliar with the term," Owen said opening his eyes.

Andras's calm voice steadied him. "A Latin term meaning *something for something*. Or we could say *what for what* or even *give and take*."

"Very well, ye go first."

Andras leaned forward, elbowed his knee and supported his chin with his knuckles. "After your tad helped me recover from my wounds, I poured over my medical journals for a remedy."

"To cure the disorder?"

"Nay, to take my life."

Stunned by his bluntness, and rendered speechless, he watched for any sign of emotion crossing

Andras's eyes. Long moments later, and absent a change in his sentiment, curiosity compelled him forward. "Ye looked for a means to end your own life?"

Still no change in his expression other than a muscle twitching in his jaw.

"Desperately and for a lengthy time."

His voice little more than a whisper Owen asked, "Why did ye change your mind?"

"Three reasons." At last, an inflection of defiance edged his words. "Traherne would not only claim the sword, but victory. Number two, 'twould be the coward's way out, and number three, the devastation on Carys's face when she realized she'd been abandoned again rose before me."

At a loss for words, Owen continued to stare at the hardened features.

"Quid pro quo, your turn."

The blood pounded in his ears and heat rose in his face from unspent anger. "I smell the blood, feel the pain as if 'tis happening again, right now." He bit his lip against the smoldering rage. "Worse, his face looms before me and his...."

The words hung in the air until Andras finished the sentence for him. "Fangs."

"Aye and I can't dispel the visions. The images steal my thoughts during the day and haunt my dreams at night."

"I wish I could promise ye the nightmares will cease. 'Twould be a fallacy, but they will abate in time."

Owen clasped his head in his hands. "While I knew of it, I never understood the blackness in ye until now. A portion of my world has been awakened to new imaginings that once lay far beyond my control, yet a coldness resides in my soul now that didn't exist before." A scream of rage at the back of his throat fought for release. "'Tis deep and dark with far-reaching roots into Dagan's Underworld."

"It will always exist, but ye are master of your own destiny. Ye decide whether to unleash the wickedness or control it."

"That's what I fear most, Andras; I won't be able to control it."

"Ye must concentrate on the strengths ye source now, not the demon ye can do nothing about. Ye're a Dyn Hysbys, a wizard, a great healer. Use this honor for the greater good."

"I'll do my best." He paused. "There's more."

The gray eyes he'd come to rely on and love softened. "Speak freely."

He nodded and squirmed in the chair. "Ye have not looked my way since we arrived here. What have I done to displease ye so?"

Long, bronze fingers reached out and brushed his knee. Andras's touch sent a jolt of hot fire pedaling through his blood. Fighting several demons borne of lust, craving, and uncontrolled desire, he could no longer harness the battles raging inside. He thirsted for blood, hungered for Andras's intimate possession, yet had been denied both since that fateful night Dagan turned him.

"Ye have done nothing to displease me, could do nothing that would turn me from ye."

A tiny spark of hope ignited. Andras still cared for him. "What then, why do ye avoid me as if I'm a leper? From others I expect it but have never been treated thus by ye."

He smiled for the first time since entering the library and Owen felt drugged by the beautiful transformation of his face. "Until ye learn to control the blood thirst 'twould be devastating for us both. A long tooth's desires are heightened during intimate contact...yours and mine. I learned how to control my cravings before I came to ye, touched ye, so what happened to me wouldn't happen to ye."

"How long before ye learned to control them?" he asked, a sense of urgency driving him. Before Andras had a chance to answer, he asked another question. "Will ye teach me, now, tonight?"

He leaned forward, even closer, until his lips almost brushed his. "Are ye attempting to seduce me?"

Owen closed his eyes and parted his lips in breathless anticipation, waiting for the kiss he longed for, needed more than the air he breathed.

Andras slapped his knee. "Seek out Bellamy in the stables and tell him to saddle two mounts." He rose from the chair, walked to the door and called out over his shoulder. "Ask him to scrounge up a pair of sturdy boots. Ye can't run down wild beasts in monk's sandals."

His heart thundered. The feral streak he'd kept so restrained inside him would soon come unleashed. His bloodlust would be quenched. Andras would teach him how to hunt down the beasts of the forest and slake his thirst.

He rose from the chair almost giddy with the thought—if he had anything to say about it, Andras would sate his hunger wrapped in his arms.

* * *

The edge of the forest gleamed with sharp reflected light from a waxing moon. Andras dismounted and motioned for Owen to do the same. He leaped from the saddle with a rush of exhilaration even though he didn't know what to expect once they entered the deep interior of the woods. He knew only this unquenchable thirst would soon be appeased.

Andras gathered the reins from both mounts and tied them to the fronds of a dense thicket of bracken. "They'll smell the horses so we walk from here."

"Will they not pick up our scent?"

"Our human scent, aye. We must use our speed to thwart them."

His words rushed out faster than he'd intended.

"Who would *them* be?"

Patient as always, Andras turned and spoke. "We hunt deer your first time.

Listen and watch me."

With a nod, Owen crept into the forest behind him; his eyes open for the slightest movement, his heightened hearing on alert. Nocturnal critters scampered around them foraging for food, and a variety of night birds shrieked a warning as they passed—sounds he recognized from prior treks into the forest but never heard with such clarity.

He thought about the night Andras saved him from Traherne. It seemed an eternity ago. His heart had hammered then too, but had strummed a beat of sheer fright, unlike the wild pummel of anticipation coursing through his chest now.

In front of him, Andras came to an abrupt halt and placed a finger to his lips. He nodded to his right, and Owen followed his gaze to a pack of wild boars scampering down a narrow path. A pungent, fetid smell wafted around him—a combination of rotten refuse, animal feces and urine. Why had he never noticed the horrific odor clinging to their hides before? He had no desire to tangle with their tusks and nasty tempers, at least not until he knew his strengths and weaknesses.

As soon as the boars passed, Andras resumed his pace, stopping again a short time later by a clearing with a stream running through the center. A large-antlered buck came into view and seconds later, his mate walked into the open. Owen saw the graceful curve of her neck, focused on the tremulous beat of the pulse in her throat.

Beside him, Andras whispered, "Watch me, and if the doe runs, keep her from the trees, force her back into the clearing."

Owen nodded and thought him a fool for putting so much faith in him, particularly when he'd done nothing to merit it, had not one lick of confidence in himself when it came to this venture.

Like a phantom lunging through the night sky, Andras struck, swift and hard. Dropping the buck with a crushing blow, he turned on the doe before she realized her mate had fallen. Birds shrieked overhead, the sound of small beasts scattering in all directions found them, and then a deafening silence fell over the woods.

Their eyes met across the clearing and Andras called him forth with a crook of his finger. Streaks of moonbeams snaked through the pines, exposing Andras's elongated teeth. Like a beacon they drew him as the scent of the doe's rich, aromatic blood and her recent death wafted around him. Owen's fangs emerged while he walked forward and focused on the gash in her neck where Andras had left his mark.

Bright, red liquid pumped from the wound. Owen fell upon her like a starved beast and slaked his lust, exalting in the rush of euphoria and the taste of her blood. At some time during his feast, he knew Andras had left his side. Caught up in a vortex of cravings, rapture and the desire to satiate his hunger, he assumed Andras had moved on to the buck when another wave of fresh blood filled his senses.

Long minutes later, he lifted his head and saw Andras staring at him, the man's thoughts unreadable. Guilt assailed him and a small measure of shame. What had he become? What had he done?

"Don't," Andras said. "I know what ye are thinking at this moment without trying to read your mind."

Owen closed his eyes and leaned back on his calves. "Will it always be like this?"

"Aye, but take comfort in knowing ye do this to spare the innocent human."

Andras walked toward him, held out his hand, and pulled him to his feet. "Come, we'll wash our shirts in the stream."

* * *

A cauldron of emotions hit Owen full force while rinsing out his shirt in the stream: confusion, mortification and, above all, a potent desire for Andras that never seemed to subside. Beside him, Andras went through the same motions of plunging his shirt into the water before retracting it, only to plunge it in again.

Other than the few words he'd spoken moments ago, the man had fallen silent and Owen couldn't begin to assess his thoughts. He had no words to curb the conflicting feelings Andras must feel, the same feelings he now owned. Andras seemed to know things others didn't at times or at the very least sense them. Mayhap his age had something to do with his calm approach to life or his compassionate nature when dealing with his fellow man. Aye, the man could be dangerous when need be but only when backed into a corner or when someone threatened those he loved.

Andras came to his feet, shucked his trousers, and removed his sturdy shoes. Then he dove into the water, and moments later, came up sputtering, his midnight hair shiny and wet.

Owen laughed and called out, "Cold?"

The promise of pleasure burned in his eyes. "Come see for yourself."

He needed no formal invitation. Rolling his trousers down his hips, he stepped out of them, removed his boots and walked into the welcoming pool. His body shivered from the brush of cool water against his naked flesh, but also from its instinctive response to Andras. It seemed it no longer belonged to him, but always to Andras since the first time he'd found pleasure in his arms.

Andras reached for him and pulled him next to his warmth. He drew his head back and bared his throat, his lips finding the pulse in the hollow of his throat, his fingers working their magic against his bare chest and nipples, seeking and exploring, pitching him into a state of oblivion.

Andras's lips traveled along the flesh of his shoulder and returned to claim his mouth. A hot flame clawed at Owen's belly when he slipped a hand beneath the water, pressed it into the small of Owen's back and pulled him close. He felt the full length of Andras against his body, wickedly arousing. Limper than a jellyfish washed up on shore, he couldn't have resisted if he'd wanted to.

Andras's tongue probed the inside of his mouth, eliciting a strangled moan from his throat. He wrapped his legs around Andras's hips and twined his fingers in his hair, reveling in the taste and feel of him. Without warning, Andras broke from the kiss and another moan echoed across the watery depths. His, he knew, but he couldn't stop it from escaping.

With Owen clinging to him like a powder monkey, Andras pushed through the water, back to shore, and laid him in the tall grass. He looked down on Owen, the silver eyes burning like bonfires along the hills of the moors. Owen couldn't think. The breeze rustling through the leaves of the mighty oaks, the soothing sound of water trickling over stones, and his own heavy breathing came to him through a funnel.

Andras dropped to his knees and, moving with efficiency, pinned Owen's arms over his head with one hand, exploring every inch of his skin with the other.

Owen's mind drifted, floated somewhere between lucidity and dreams. How had he been so fortunate to meet Andras? What great deed had he done in life to deserve such bliss?

On his knees, Andras straddled him and moved his hand beneath his hips, lifting them to meet his. "This will be a night for first times. I'm going to take ye like this so I can look into your eyes while I claim ye."

Owen gasped at the depth of passion in the silver mirrors.

"Say it, Owen, say ye want me."

"When have ye ever doubted it?"

"I long to hear ye say it; need to know your love is not borne of loneliness or vulnerability."

"I want ye, Andras, have wanted ye from the moment I first saw your face." Duw help him, he did. He couldn't fight it, even if it was wrong to love another man. He pulled his head down until Andras's mouth lingered near his. "I want the forgetfulness that only ye can summon; I long to travel to that place where only your hard body can take me."

Andras's fingers traced the outline of his lips and he spoke, his voice clear, so real, Owen lost pace with his breathing. "Ah, I want all of ye too, your mouth, your skin, and every inch of your body."

The moon hung above them, pale white like the stars. Nothing moved or breathed in the universe but the passion between them. Andras released his wrists and cupped his hips before entering him.

Owen strained beneath him, that magnificent body driving into him time and again. Soaring to heights he never dreamed existed, his body one with Andras's, he rose to meet him. Desire overrode everything else, obliterated his every thought as his soul-starved senses cried out his hunger. Standing at the edge of a great crevice, Owen stepped into the open air and spiraled down...down...down. His release came hard and fierce. Silver flashes of lightning coursed through the sky and shattered him. Calling out Owen's name with one final thrust, Andras wrung the last strains of passions from his drenched body.

For a timeless moment, Owen looked into Andras's soul. He'd whisper his name with his dying breath. No matter what happened in the future, if he disappeared from this life, if a thousand years passed, the last word to fall from his lips would be Andras.

Epilogue

At the evening meal that night, Uncle Maxen was his usual jovial self, reciting the latest quatrains he'd collected during his recent trip to London.

Owen and Carys laughed until their bellies ached before Carys cajoled the elderly man into talking about her favorite subject.

"Tell us again about the knockers, Uncle Maxen," she said wide-eyed.

"Oh, they're the most devilish creatures ye will ever encounter. Two feet tall and grizzled, they live in the mines beneath the ground. Dressed like the miners themselves, they spend their days making mischief; they steal their tools and their food when they're not looking."

"The elders say they knock on the walls to get them to collapse."

"I don't believe 'tis true. The knockers are harmless practical jokers who toil endlessly but never finish a task."

Soon the discussion turned to the history of Sycharth Castle and the ancestor who first owned the infamous sword.

Carys retrieved a sheaf of paper from the sideboard and with great fanfare read aloud from a document written by Owain Glyn Dwr's Court poet, Iolo Gocha. "The landscape includes a rabbit warren, deer park, meadows and hayfields, a mill on a smooth-flowing stream and a fish pond abounding in pike and splendid whiting."

It seemed natural after the stimulating discussion they'd take a walk at sunset to look over the earthwork remains of Sycharth's old motte and bailey, its contours now disguised by a cluster of trees and overgrown vegetation.

While Andras, Maxen and Carys continued their conversation about the history of the noble house, Owen stood at the crown of the motte and fought the lightheaded feeling that found him. A fine bead of sweat broke out on his forehead and his mouth went dry.

Although aware the others surrounded him, he lapsed into trance-like state, the indomitable feeling of another time and place overwhelming him. Morose visions of annihilation, destruction and death crept into the dark recesses of his mind. Horses screamed, and wounded men littered a smoke-filled battlefield.

An unbreakable bond between him and the land beneath his feet stretched across centuries, the force of energy so potent it stole his breath. Breaching years, forging boundaries and time, it called to him. A distant voice from a violent past broke the barrier, the voice so pure, so intelligible, he looked to his side expecting to see the person standing there.

Andras's voice pushed through the tunnel of history, "Owen, are ye well?"

He looked at the ground at his feet and felt his brow furrow when a visualization of a sword surfaced—not just any sword, the Prince's sword.

"Owen." Andras's voice grew louder as he walked toward him. "Have ye taken ill?"

He shook his head. "Nay, not ill." Recovering his wits, he forced a hesitant smile.

"Pardon me, I must see to something back at the manor."

He couldn't remain on the motte. The longer he stood there, the more lethal the dark forces became, twisting and writhing around him like pit vipers from the gates of Hades. He saw Andras cloaked in black, his long hair fanned out in the wind, the sword in his hand braced against a tormented sky. Dark demons swarmed above him; their ghoulish faces masked in death.

Owen struggled to breathe and barely made it to his bedchamber before he lost his evening meal in the porcelain bowl on his bureau. He clutched his stomach, crawled to the bed and dragged his body up, collapsing onto the feather-tick mattress.

Curling up into a ball, he willed the malevolent foreboding to leave, closed his eyes and sought the sweet nothingness of the dream world.

* * *

Strong arms drew him against a warm welcoming body and moments later Andras's warm breath whispered against his ear. "What happened out there on the motte this evening?"

At first, Owen wondered if he'd dreamed the entire affair. Andras's solemn words confirmed he hadn't. "I'm at a loss to explain it."

"Try."

"'Twas so dark, so evil, I have no desire to return, not even in my thoughts."

"Another nightmare about Dagan?"

"Nay, not of him, and yet...."

His voice tight with concern, Andras pressed him. "And yet?"

"Others like him."

"The insufferable ones?"

He nodded and expelled a long breath. "Not here and yet here, in this place, the motte, the bailey, I saw it all."

"Shush, don't think of it now," he said his voice drifting into a hushed whisper.

A shiver ran down his spine. "Ye were there, Andras. I saw ye in combat against the vampires." His chest felt as if it would burst when the next medley of images flashed behind his eyes. "Ye battled another plague-spotted creature, an abomination to Duw's kingdom and all that is holy."

He said the words tentatively, as if he wanted to diffuse the panic enveloping him.

"What could be more sinister than vampires and werewolves?"

"A foul beast, the likes of which I've seen in my tad's picture books."

"Ye have seen such a being?"

"Aye."

"Does it possess a name?"

When he spoke, his voice wavered. "Draig, the most cursed dragon to ever spit fire."

Andras grew still, the only sound from his lips, his steady breathing. A short time later, he turned Owen around until they lay face to face. "I don't know what it means but whatever happens now, in the future, we'll face it together, as one."

Owen touched his face. "Are ye certain?"

"More certain than I've ever been of anything in my life."

If only Owen could steal a portion of Andras's strength, his formidable courage.

"Sleep now, no harm will come to ye."

Owen closed his eyes, knowing when he opened them. he'd still be wrapped in the shelter of Andras's arms.

Tonight, the vampire wouldn't vanish like the morning mist.

THE END

About the Author

Keta Diablo lives in the Midwest part of the United States on six acres of gorgeous woodland. When she isn't writing or gardening, she loves to commune with nature. A pair of barn owls returns to the property every year to birth their young and show them off in the high branches of the oak trees. Nothing more adorable than these white fluffy babies with heart-shaped faces. A lifelong animal lover, Keta devotes her time and support to the local animal shelter. Emma LaPounce, a rescued feline, has been her furry companion for the last ten years.

Keta is an award-winning and bestselling author who writes in several genres: Western Romance, Historical Romance, Paranormal Romance and Contemporary Romance. In a past life, she wrote Gay Romance. Her books have received numerous accolades, including RWA contest finalist, Authors After Dark finalist, Top Pick of the Month and Recommended Review from many top review sites, and Best Romance Finalist from The Independent Author Network.

Ps: For some strange reason, ghosts often show up in her stories, no matter the genre.

Keta would love to have you follow visit her blog to see her other books:
http://ketaskeep.blogspot.com

Made in the USA
Las Vegas, NV
21 August 2021